"What brought you back east? Senior year seems like a strange time to transfer." He opened a package of pens and slid them into a coffee mug next to the books before dropping the packaging in the small trash can beside his desk.

Inside my head, I saw Viktor—his cheeks sunken in, his skin pale and sickly. He looked like I'd feared he would look when I first saw him upon my return. Attached to his arms were tubes. Covering the table beside him were bottles of pills. The image of my parents' lab flashed through my mind, too. I swore I could smell the burnt remains. Then there was Grace, sitting there all prim and proper. In her hands were the pages from my father's journal. The corner of her mouth lifted in a sadistic smirk. Shaking off the daydream with a shiver, I said, "Family stuff."

ALSO BY ZAC BREWER

The Cemetery Boys

Madness

The Legacy of Tril: Soulbound

THE CHRONICLES OF VLADIMIR TOD

Eighth Grade Bites

Ninth Grade Slays

Tenth Grade Bleeds

Eleventh Grade Burns

Twelfth Grade Kills

THE SLAYER CHRONICLES

First Kill

Second Chance

Third Strike

The BLOOD BETWEEN US

ZAC BREWER

HARPER TEEN

An imprint of HarperCollinsPublishers

HarperTeen is an imprint of HarperCollins Publishers.

The Blood Between Us
Copyright © 2016 by Zac Brewer
www.epicreads.com

Library of Congress Control Number: 2015947484
ISBN 978-0-06-230792-7

Typography by Carla Weise
17 18 19 20 21   PC/LSCH   10 9 8 7 6 5 4 3 2 1
❖
First paperback edition, 2017

To Maggie Preiss,
whose spirit still roams the halls
of Spencer Road Branch Library, I'm sure

CHAPTER 1

ABSOLUTE ZERO:

The lowest temperature possible, at which particles are essentially stationary

There's nothing like the acrid smell of a building on fire. Even once the flames have been extinguished and the smoke has withered into nothingness, the smell permeates everything. The burned remains that the fire didn't claim. The air that hangs above the hollowed, blackened walls. The clothing of anyone who was unfortunate enough to be nearby. The fire doesn't just smell, either. It has a taste.

No one thinks about that. The taste of a house fire. It tastes sour. Bitter, even.

I wasn't surprised to get called out of my eighth-grade lit class to the headmaster's office that morning—not when

I realized that my sister, Grace, had been called in, too. The two of us were always getting lectured on our behavior toward each other. But that morning, as I tried to think of what I had done or said about her recently so I could prepare my defense, nothing came to mind.

When I walked in, she didn't even glance in my direction. Her ankles were crossed, her hands folded neatly in her lap. There wasn't a single wrinkle on her school uniform. Every pleat of her navy skirt was in order; her gray cardigan was buttoned precisely over her white blouse. The front of her long, black hair was pinned neatly back with a single silver barrette—the rest lay in ringlets on her thin shoulders. She was the picture of perfection, making every effort to live up to her name. It kind of made me nauseous. We didn't speak. We rarely did, because when we actually made the effort, it inevitably ended in an argument. It had always been that way between us. Some things just were.

In contrast to Grace's flawless exterior, I couldn't care less about appearances. My uniform jacket was wrinkled, its sleeves rolled up and pushed to just below my elbows. I'd once again passed on the required polished oxford shoes for a pair of Chucks that had seen better days. My hair was disheveled and longer than the dean allowed in his thick book of rules. But some things were worth a few demerits. And if the Wills Institute was so concerned about outward appearance that they would actually kick out a student because of his shoes, then so be it. At least then I wouldn't have to look at Grace's smug face anymore.

I scratched my head and yawned, my black hair sticking up haphazardly with the distinct air of not giving a crap. Funnily enough, I mused, our hair color was the only thing Grace and I really had in common. Maybe that's why our parents had chosen me for adoption—because I had at least one obvious physical trait like my adoptive sister, which might make people ask fewer questions about my heritage. Or maybe they'd walked into the adoption agency and chosen me at random. I didn't know. What I did know was that my parents had loved me just as much as my sister for as long as I could remember—adoption or no adoption—despite what Grace might have said otherwise.

The clock on the wall was the only thing in the room making a sound, and its constant ticking was driving me crazy. Crazy enough to attempt to engage in conversation with Grace. Sighing, I rolled my head to the side and looked at my sister again. "So what'd you do this time?"

Other than the slight twitch in her left cheek, she gave no indication that she had heard a word I'd said. It wasn't a surprise. Grace was only ever semipolite to me when she was forced to be.

Mrs. Noonan, the headmaster's secretary, opened the

door to his office and said, "Headmaster Snelgrove will see you both now."

Grace stood, took a moment to straighten her skirt, and stepped forward with her head held high. I dragged myself from my chair, dreading every moment of whatever conversation was waiting for us on the other side of that door. Once Grace stepped inside, I stood and followed, muttering under my breath, "Nice talking to ya, sis."

There were two leather club chairs on the receiving side of the headmaster's desk, and I'd spent so much time in here, I even had a favorite. So naturally, when I walked into the room, I found Grace sitting in it. I bumped the chair—not accidentally—on my way to the other one, inciting a glare from her. Yeah, I'd pay for that one later.

The headmaster was sitting on the authoritative side of the desk, and when he looked up at us, everything that I thought this conversation would be about blew away like ash in the wind. The familiar chastising look in his eyes was gone, replaced by sorrow and regret. Something had happened. Something terrible.

I looked at Grace, and in a moment that I would never forget, she looked back at me in absolute understanding. Before the headmaster could even speak, we knew our parents were dead.

"Grace. Adrien. It's good to see you again." He cleared

his throat and glanced around the room, as if the words that he was searching for had been carved in the dark wood paneling of the walls. But there were no words there, just as there were no words on my tongue. I wasn't sure how I knew that my parents were dead, exactly. It was just this sinking, terrible, black-hole sensation at the center of my chest. I felt like I was collapsing into myself, like if I were to succumb to the feeling of dread that was spreading out from my center down my limbs, I might cease to exist. My psychiatrist might point out that I was having a panic attack, or that I was prone to such jumps in thought and emotion due to my anxiety, but I knew that this time it was more than that. My parents—our parents, to be fair—were gone.

The headmaster opened a drawer on the right side of his desk and retrieved a box of tissues. He set the box on his desk, but neither of us made a move for it. There was no room for tears. Only the desert of shock and dread.

The headmaster cleared his throat again, and, finally, he got down to business. "I wish that we were meeting under better circumstances. I'm afraid that I have some terrible news. It seems that there was an accident. Involving your parents. Your father and mother . . . they didn't survive. I'm so sorry."

I swallowed, but every bit of moisture in my mouth had evaporated. I couldn't form words. My entire vocabulary had been consumed by my grief. There was nothing more to say.

Grace spoke, her voice just as calm and even as ever. Hearing it made my heart rate pick up in anger. "What exactly happened? An accident in the lab?"

How could she be calm at a time like this? But there she was, poised, even camera ready, her tone the same as if she were inquiring about her grade on a recent chemistry test.

"Why would you assume that? It could have been any-thing. A car accident. An armed robbery. Why would you assume it was in the lab?" But as the words left my mouth, that little voice at the back of my mind whispered its own poignant question, *How did I know they were dead before the headmaster said anything?*

"Actually, Grace's instincts are exactly on point. As far as I've been informed, there was some sort of explosion." He shuffled a stack of papers around on his desk. "Your god-father has sent word that he'll be here to gather you both this afternoon. You should go to your dormitories and pack. You may await his arrival in the main office. Mrs. Noonan will give you your temporary absence paperwork. I'm sure Viktor will take care of everything that you need from here on. But if there is anything at all that I or my staff can—"

"What about midterms?" If it was possible to do so, Grace sat up even straighter. Sometimes I wondered if she was a Vulcan from Star Trek. All logic, no emotion. It bothered me. I wasn't exactly reaching for the tissue box, either, but still, I couldn't deny that there was a hole in me, this horrible emptiness. It was obvious that Grace felt nothing but concern for herself. The headmaster was looking at her in a kind of surprised daze. Grace said, "They're next week. How long will we be gone?"

After a pause, he said, "You are, of course, welcome to return to class when you're ready, Ms. Dane. But I would hope that you'd consider taking some time away from your studies to properly grieve."

"What the hell is wrong with you?"

She snapped her eyes to me when I spoke, as if she'd been suddenly dropped into an ice bucket of disbelief that someone would dare accuse her of being anything other than perfect. I leaned toward her and chose my words carefully, but coldly. "They're *dead*, Grace. Mom and Dad are dead. And you're seriously worried about midterms? Our parents are gone. *Forever.*"

She drew her arms up around her and pulled her gaze away from mine. "I was just asking."

My jaw tightened until the ache spread up the sides of my face.

Headmaster Snelgrove kept his voice calm, but stern. "Arrangements can be made for any make-up work, should either of you desire. But right now, we think it's best that you each take the time you need. And, of course, when you are ready to return, our counseling staff is completely at your disposal."

There were other words, kind words, but I heard none of them. The screeching sound of my pain was growing too quickly to allow anything else inside my mind. Dead. My parents were dead. The only parents I had ever known. My father. My mother. The people who had picked me out of all the other kids to adopt. I was now thirteen. And an orphan. Again.

An hour later, we were both standing outside in front of the main entrance—a no-doubt neatly packed suitcase in Grace's hand, a stuffed duffel bag in mine. I remember I hadn't really packed. It had been more like going through the motions, gathering items, shoving them into a bag, and not thinking much about what they were or what I might need. I was in pure survival mode.

When Viktor's car pulled up, a new sense of dread filled me. What would life be like now, with him and Julian as my guardians? Who would be my family? Them? Grace?

Viktor opened the driver's side door and stepped out of the car. He still looked as he had the last night I'd seen him, over Thanksgiving break. Handsome, with his dark hair and bright blue eyes. He was wearing a suit—something

I'd never seen him without. There had always been a sense of formality to Viktor, a sense of obligation to impress. It reminded me of Grace.

His face was drawn as he helped us put our bags in the trunk. "I'm so terribly sorry, children. I'm not sure what could have gone wrong. But please know that I will be here for you whenever you need me."

He closed the trunk with a thud and placed his hands on our shoulders. His eyes met ours in turn as he spoke. "I'm your legal guardian now, so I mean that in any sense. I've known you since you were this high, and we've always been as close as family. That's true now more than ever. I want to help you however I can."

With a squeeze and one last, meaningful look at each of us, Viktor let go and moved toward the driver's door. "Shall we go? I thought it best that you stay with me until after the funeral. Longer, if either of you prefers. Whatever I can do . . ."

"Take us home, Viktor." The words left my mouth before I could even really think them. But once I did, I knew that was exactly what I needed—where I needed to be.

Viktor nodded, not understanding. "Of course."

"To *our* home." Viktor met my gaze and furrowed his brow in confusion and sorrow. I could feel my bottom lip shaking, but refused to let tears fall. Crying wouldn't solve anything. "I want to see the lab. I want to see where they died."

Grace's hand was on the passenger's side door handle. As she opened the door, she shot me a glare. "You're being ridiculous."

But I didn't think I was being ridiculous at all. "Aren't you even a tiny bit curious?"

"Morbid. That's what this is, Adrien. Can't you at least wait until their bodies are cold before you go making this all about you?" Her eyes were bright with anger.

I remember when we were nine and I broke my arm falling off the tree house ladder. Grace went on and on about how I'd almost landed right on her head. According to Grace, I could've killed her if I had—broken her neck or something. According to her, she'd barely managed to jump out of my way in time. Never mind my broken arm and that stupid cast that I was forced to wear for eight weeks. The whole thing was so damn traumatic for Grace that it was the subject of every conversation that summer.

Of course, she failed to mention that the only reason I'd fallen was because she was shaking the ladder.

"Children, please." Viktor held up a hand, stopping the argument before it had really begun. "Grace, I'd be happy to take you to my home and then drive Adrien to see the lab.

I'm sure the investigators will have all they need by the time we arrive. But if not, please don't make a scene, Adrien. They need time to gather evidence."

"I can't believe you're giving in to his whims, Uncle." While Viktor was our godfather, he was not any blood relation to our parents. He had been our father's best friend in college, and they had remained close ever since. He was the closest thing to family we had, now that our parents were gone. But Grace had taken to calling him Uncle several years before that day. It was just one more way for her to push me away. She shook her head and slid into her seat, closing the door a little harder than it required.

I slid into the backseat behind Viktor. Once the engine was running, Viktor said, "We all mourn in our own ways. While some of us require time to gather our thoughts and wrap our minds around whatever feelings our heart may hold—"

"Or time to realize that having a heart and feelings is something that humans were meant to do." Viktor ignored the words that I had spoken under my breath.

"—Some of us flit about like hummingbirds, gathering nectar from here and there, trying to find some connection, to make sense of it all. Your brother is the latter, Grace. And there is absolutely nothing wrong with it."

The rest of the car ride was silent. When we pulled up

to Viktor's massive home and the car came to a stop, Grace simply opened the door and got out. Julian, Viktor's partner, was waiting at the front door to greet us. I couldn't hear what it was that Grace said to him, but I could tell the tone that she had used to say it by her body language. She stomped off, disappearing through the front door. She was angry. Maybe hurt. I couldn't care less.

Viktor waved to Julian before putting the car in gear and pulling away from the house. He caught my eye in the rear-view mirror. "There is also nothing wrong with the way that your sister is facing her grief, Adrien. Be gentle with her. She's more sensitive than you may realize. And you need each other, now more than ever."

"There was a time when I needed her, Viktor. But she's spent years making her feelings about me perfectly clear. Now I just need her to stay out of my way." I sank down in my seat and watched the familiar scenery as we passed trees, mailboxes, houses, and fields. I was going home. For the very last time.

That's when the smell of the house fire reached me—long before the sight of it did. It smelled like decay. It smelled like the aftermath of war. And like a soldier stumbling upon a grisly scene on the battlefield, I didn't want to look, didn't want to see the source of the stench—I *had* to see it.

The car shifted to the right, curving around the bend. As

we turned, I found myself unable to breathe. I knew that just around that curve, I would be able to see my home, and I was terrified of what awaited me. Time seemed to slow, and my head filled with horrific images of the house in ashes and rubble, our furniture and walls merely charred remains . . . and poking up from the center of the pile, a thin, pale arm. My mother's arm. Her index finger pointed crookedly up at the sky.

My lungs burned from holding my breath, and when I finally let myself exhale and inhale again, my nostrils burned.

But then we rounded the corner, and our home greeted me as it always had. Tall, white, surrounded by perfectly manicured flower beds. I scanned the building, but couldn't see where the fire had done any damage. Viktor pulled the car into the circle drive and put it in park. As if guessing what I'd been thinking, he said, "The damage was largely contained in the lab and the back of the house."

As I reached for the door handle, Viktor met my eyes in the rearview mirror. "Adrien. Are you certain you want to do this?"

"Wait here." I opened the door and stepped out onto the driveway. The gravel crunched beneath my sneakers as I walked away from the car, leaving Viktor in the driver's seat. This was something I had to do, and I had to do it alone.

I passed Maggie on my way to the house—my father's gorgeous black 1972 Oldsmobile Cutlass 442 coupe—and tried not to look inside at her worn leather interior. I had spent countless hours in that car . . . and under the car, too. She was the embodiment of my time alone with my dad. The lab had represented both my parents, but the car . . . that was my father and my father alone. My dad had been an Olds man for as long as I had known him. And, apart from my mother, Maggie had been the love of his life.

Even now I can imagine the look in my father's eyes whenever he'd pick up Maggie's keys or change her oil. She was beautifully flawed and his most prized possession. And I got the feeling it had gone the other way around as well. Maggie had loved my father deeply. How would she fare without him now? How would I?

I rounded the right side of the house, and the full impact of the fire hit me. The screened-in back porch, where Dad would read in the summer while Mom tended to her orchids, had been completely obliterated. It lay in ashes, and where the fire had stopped at the main house looked reminiscent of an enormous black bite mark. As if the fire, the explosion, had taken a bite out of our lives and gobbled my parents whole.

I continued, my steps more urgent, around the back of the house to the extension that my parents had added a few years ago—their lab. Or rather, where their lab had been the last time I'd been home. It wasn't there anymore. Just ash and soot and the melted remnants of equipment and experiments.

When I lifted my eyes from the lab, I got the full view of the house, and my heart sank even farther into my stomach. The back of the house stood open to the elements, its insides blackened like the rotten core of an apple. I climbed the rubble to the house and then pulled myself up onto the main floor until I was standing in the breakfast nook. A glass of water, its contents now black, sat on the table. The kitchen still looked as it had the last time I'd stepped into it. Only now it was a ruined memory.

My lungs grew tighter with every step. The heat from the fire had melted our television set. The spines of the books in the bookcase next to it were all stained from smoke. I reached for my mother's autographed copy of *Carrie*. It had been a gift to her from my father. Her favorite book autographed by her favorite author. Somehow, its spine was cleaner than the rest, like some special force field had protected it from the smoke damage. When I lifted the book from the shelf, another tome caught my eye. It was my father's journal, just where it had always been when it wasn't in use. Every detail of his biggest project—his life's dream—was contained within the pages of this book. His notes filled every page, and where his stopped, my mother's notes began. They had been a team, the two of them. Intelligent minds, both.

His research was brilliant and had so many potential applications, both in the military and out. With my mother's input on bioluminescent plants, he was well on his way to developing eye drops that would allow the user to see in the dark, eliminating the need for costly night vision goggles and enabling underwater explorers to see more broadly in their ocean expeditions. His invention would reduce costs across the board and change the world forever. It would save lives.

Only now the journal was covered with soot and the stain of unfinished progress. I picked up the book and shook the droplets of water and debris from its cover. It was coming with me. I couldn't leave it here. I could leave almost anything, but not this.

On the next shelf up was a family photo we'd just had done a few weeks before. I took it down and wiped the soot from the glass. Grace and I sat in chairs in front of our parents. My father stood to my mother's left, his hand placed awkwardly on her shoulder. Anyone else looking at the photo might have seen a nice, normal family. But I could see the grimace on my mother's lips at my father's touch. I could see the way that Grace's chair had been moved just slightly away from mine right before the photo was taken. We were all dressed in our finest, but no one seemed happy. The look in my parents' eyes was one of pain. The look in mine was confusion. Grace sat stoic—a perfect statue in a garden of chaos.

The morning of that photo had been very tense. My parents had been arguing after some woman had come to the front door and my father had told her to leave. I stood in the foyer, listening to the words that were hurled back and forth between my mom and dad, but not really understanding them. What I did understand was the expression on my mother's face when she noticed me. She wanted me to leave. So that's just what I did.

That afternoon, we'd ridden in silence to the photographer's studio. Fight or no fight, my dad wasn't one to miss an appointment. I didn't speak while we were getting arranged into the perfect family pose. All I kept thinking about was the look in my mom's eyes when she'd noticed me eavesdropping that morning, and how much it had hurt to wonder if she'd regretted adopting me.

Strange where your mind takes you sometimes. Their argument wasn't about me—I don't think so, anyway—but I brought it to that place regardless.

I returned the photo to the shelf, laying it facedown.

Without allowing myself to set foot upstairs or to give

myself over to the pain that was burning its way up from the depths of my soul, I opened the front door and stepped outside. My mind was blank. They were dead. They were really dead. What would I do now? Who would be my family?

I don't remember sliding into the passenger seat of Viktor's car or closing the door. The next thing I knew, we were barreling down the road back to Viktor's house, and I was clutching the journal to my chest, not caring that I'd never get the smell of the fire out of my school uniform . . . or out of my memory.

As we pulled through the gate onto Viktor's long, paved driveway, I flipped through the journal. My thumb stopped at a spot two-thirds of the way in, where I could see that several pages had been torn from the book. My father was a brilliant scientist, but he did have his quirks. One of those quirks was that he tended to be a bit obsessive-compulsive when it came to his work. The way he took notes was all about order and precision. He would just as soon toss a journal out and get a new one than damage one and continue to work in it. So what had happened to these pages? Someone must have taken them, but who?

The car came to a stop in front of the redbrick house, and I glanced up at a window on the second floor. Grace was standing there, looking out through the glass, watching the car like she was sad to see us return. I set my jaw as I exited the car, and Grace met my eyes with a snarl.

I didn't know what her problem was.

Viktor called to me from the back of the car. "Adrien, why don't you help me out with these bags?"

Before I could react, Grace's suitcase came flying through the air toward me. I stepped aside and let it sail past. I was more than happy to carry my own bag, but there was no way I was doing anything for her.

The suitcase popped open when it hit the ground. Grace's clothes were scattered all over the driveway. From the look on his face, I could tell that Viktor was not nearly as amused as I was. Reluctantly, I started picking up the mess. That's when I saw it. A small, yellowed piece of paper. There was no writing on it, but I recognized that paper immediately.

I opened my father's journal and slipped the blank paper into place. The tear on the side of the paper from my sister's suitcase matched one of the missing pages in the journal perfectly. Grace had taken the pages. I had no idea where the others were or why she had them, but I was damn well going to find out.

Viktor's home was lovely and large—the perfect place to hold a memorial service for my parents, Allen and Claudia Dane. Two of the world's most brilliant scientists, or at least they were in my mind. I had foolishly thought there would be a funeral, with bodies. But the fire had been so hot that there was nothing much left of our parents' remains to put in a coffin. Rightly, and horrifically, what remains were found and identified were cremated. On the day of the service, I was sitting on the arm of the loveseat in Viktor's great room, staring at the two urns on the mantel.

Grace was on the other side of the room, a cup of steaming tea in her hand, chatting with family members I only recognized from photographs. She was dressed in a tasteful black skirt and a dark blue blouse, her flowing black curls twisted into a tight bun at the back of her head. Even in grief, she was perfectly put together. I, meanwhile, felt woefully underdressed. I'd pulled a pair of black slacks from my duffel bag that morning but hadn't ironed them, and then had thrown on a dark gray V-neck sweater. It was good enough. Dad would have said it was good enough. Besides, I doubted the dead really gave much of a crap over what people were wearing when they came to stare at the jars that held their remains.

Slipping my cell phone from my pants pocket, I noted the time and wished it would inch along a little faster. Several texts were waiting for me to respond, but they would have to wait. Right now, I just wanted to be left alone.

As quietly as I could manage, I slipped off the arm of the loveseat and made my way to the stairs. But just as I was about to get away, a familiar voice whispered harshly to me, "Where do you think you're going?"

Turning to meet my sister's bitter gaze, I rolled my eyes. "Upstairs. What's it look like?"

"You're supposed to talk to people. You haven't spoken to anyone. I'm doing *everything*." Her last word came out biting, but I didn't flinch.

Everything. Because there was so much to do when it came to staring at jars filled with ash and munching on appetizers. I sighed. "And you're doing a fine job of it, too."

"Adrien." For a moment, her voice sounded eerily like Mom's did whenever she meant business. The sound of it startled me slightly.

"What do you want me to do?"

She looked aghast. "Talk to people. Share memories with them about Mom and Dad. Act like a normal person for once."

I shrugged. "Why should I talk to anyone? They're not here to see me. They're here to look at urns."

"Because it might help them to feel better."

"Make them feel better? I don't give a damn about making them feel better, Grace. They didn't just lose their parents in a freak explosion. They didn't just have the only family they've ever known ripped away from them, leaving them with nothing but a heartless, robotic b—" I cut my words off the moment I noticed Viktor watching us from the other room. I wouldn't regret calling Grace the word that was locked inside my mind, but I might regret letting him overhear it.

My voice caught in my throat. "Who's going to help me?"

"Help yourself." She practically spit the words in my direction.

"That's what I was doing before you so rudely interrupted me." I took two steps up before pausing and looking back at her. "But while I have your attention: I know you took those pages from Dad's journal. I want them back."

"No."

I raised an eyebrow. I'd half expected her to ask me what I was talking about. "So you don't deny you took them?"

"I have no reason to keep secrets. Do you?" She folded her arms and stared me down.

"Why did you take those pages? What's on them?" I could feel the heat rising in my face.

"That is none of your business."

"What do you mean?" I took a step closer to her.

"Let's just say it's a family matter." She pointed toward the group of people in the living room. "Now get your butt back in that room and play the gracious host."

"You're a real piece of work, Grace." Turning away, I continued my ascent.

As I reached the top of the staircase, she said, "Yes.

I suppose I am. But at least I have the decency to treat our guests with the respect they deserve at a funeral."

"Memorial service. There wasn't enough of Mom and Dad left for a funeral. Remember?" I continued down the hall without so much as another glance back in her direction.

Twenty minutes later, as I lay submerged in hot water up to my chin in a large slipper tub, a soft knock came at the door. My godfather's voice soon followed. "Adrien? Might I have a word with you when you're finished?"

"You can come in, Viktor. I'm dressed." And dressed I was. Still wearing my slacks, my sweater, my shoes and socks. But soaking in a tub and wishing the world away. For how long, I wasn't sure. Maybe forever. Maybe just for the moment.

The door swung open slowly and Viktor popped his head in before stepping fully inside and closing the door behind him. He looked down at me and, grabbing a stool from the vanity, took a seat beside the tub. "It would seem you've forgotten an important step in the bathing process. Most people remove their clothing before getting into the water. Are you all right?"

"No." My words were flat as they left my lips. No feeling, no pain. They just were—the way that gravity was. Existing. But not something anyone ever really gave much thought to.

"No. I'm not all right. I'm not exactly sure what I am. But I'm most definitely not all right."

Viktor's frown deepened. "Perhaps you should stay with Julian and me for a while, until you can grieve and get your head around all that's happened."

I shook my head slowly. "No. I want to go back to school. Only . . ."

"Only what?"

I met Viktor's eyes, the lump in my throat growing exponentially. How could I tell him what I wanted to do? How could I take from him another family member, when he'd just lost my parents, too? I swallowed hard, finding my courage in the warmth of the water. "Only I don't want to go back to the Wills Institute. I want to go somewhere else. A different boarding school, far away from here. Is that okay?"

Viktor didn't miss a beat. He had always been that way—supportive, at a moment's notice. It was one of the many things that I had always admired about him. "It's perfectly all right. If that's what you want. But can I ask why?"

I sank down into the water some more until it was covering my chin. "I want to be as far away from Grace as I can possibly get."

Viktor grew silent for a moment. From the look in his eyes, I could tell that he wasn't surprised by my request, just disappointed in it. "I see."

"No, you don't. You think I'm pushing away the only family that I have left because I'm in mourning or something. But that's not it. Grace may be my adopted sister, but she's not family to me, Viktor. She's not even human. Has she shed a single tear since finding out Mom and Dad died?" I knew I was raising my voice, but I didn't care.

"Have you?" Viktor's words gave me a start. When he continued, he placed a hand on my shoulder, his fingers dipping into the water. "I'm just saying, we all grieve—"

"I know, I know. We all grieve in our own ways." I rolled my eyes. "She cried buckets in the common room when she got the letter saying her stupid hamster died. And last year when that girl in our class died in a car accident, she was almost inconsolable at her funeral. They weren't even friends, Viktor. The only difference between then and now is that no one popular is watching this time. As soon as we get back to school . . . you just wait. The waterworks will be in full service then."

I was just so done with this place. So done with my sister and the way that she was. "She hates me, y'know. She always has. From the first moment Mom and Dad brought me home, she's made her feelings toward me very clear. She's not normal."

Viktor pulled his hand from my shoulder and dried it on

a nearby towel. "There is no such thing as 'normal.' But yes, I suppose your sister is unusual. You both are. Extremely gifted, intelligent, curious young minds. Of course, it would be nice if you'd apply yourself more, so that the rest of the world could see what I see. What your parents saw. You're better than Cs, Adrien."

I frowned. "Are we really going to have this conversation now, Viktor?"

He stood up and walked over to the basin, putting the towel on the counter. He turned around, leaning against the cabinet. "There aren't many thirteen-year-olds who could carry themselves through school while living away from their parents with barely a casual shrug. In that regard, neither of you is so-called normal. I think that's why you struggle to get along. You're so similar, but neither of you can see those similarities. Grace dives into her work, hiding between the pages of her textbooks. You hide in the only way you know how, by defiantly refusing to apply yourself. But the truth is, Adrien, you're just as bright as your sister."

I couldn't take any more. I sank down into the water, letting it cover my head. Bubbles escaped my lips as I blew air out of them. I hoped that by sheer force of will I might be able to trigger some dormant gene that had lingered hidden in human DNA ever since we evolved from slimy swamp creatures, and spontaneously develop gills.

Before long, I felt Viktor's hand in my hair, gently pulling me back into the world of the air breathers. As if there had been no interruption at all, he continued, "It's like placing magnets together, end to end. They're two of the same exact thing, but they resist being close to each other. Why?"

A heavy sigh escaped my lungs. "If you're looking for the scientific explanation, it's because of their polarity. But to follow your metaphor, they resist each other because, on the atomic level, the particles that make up the metal in the magnets are incompatible. The subatomic particles push against one another until the movement creates enough force to push the other magnet away. Much like Grace has been pushing me away our entire lives."

His voice quieted for a moment. "But it's only the like poles that repel each other. You see what I'm saying?"

"It's not like I didn't try with Grace when we were kids. I wanted a sister. I wanted a family. But she kept pushing me out. I did everything I could think of to earn her approval, her affection. But she cut me off at every turn. And now that Mom and Dad are gone, I'm done. I just can't try anymore. I want to be away from her, Viktor. I need to." I held his gaze with determination, refusing to budge on the issue.

Viktor sighed, at last giving in to my request. Supportive, as always, even when he didn't really agree. "If that's what you think you need for the moment, I'll make the necessary arrangements. But I do hope this arrangement is a temporary one."

"Don't count on it."

As Viktor stood and moved back out the door, I pulled the plug on the tub and watched the water swirl into a vortex and down the drain.

That was four years ago. I haven't forgotten a thing.

CHAPTER 2

ACTIVATED COMPLEX:

A transitional structure that forms between the reactants of a chemical reaction and breaks down to form the products

I stepped out of the locker room shower and toweled off before dressing in my street clothes and heading back to my dorm room. It was the Thursday before classes started, and I figured I was safe not wearing my uniform around campus, at least until Monday. Four years later, and some things hadn't changed.

Some of the guys from the lacrosse team were meeting down at Sheggy's for burgers before catching the latest sequel in our favorite horror movie franchise, *Psycho Slasher Chainsaw Guy from Hell: Redemption*.

Stacy smiled and said hi as I passed through the common

room. She was nice. A little too nice sometimes, like we were good friends instead of casual acquaintances. But that's just how girls were, I guess. I smiled back.

It was amazing what four years away from my old life had done. True to his word, Viktor had arranged for me to enroll at a boarding school in southern California, just outside of San Diego. From my first week here, I'd felt lighter, happier, more at ease with myself. The move had been good for me. Hell, even my grades had improved.

Kind of.

For four years, I'd spent summers with friends, occasionally enjoyed a visit from Viktor and Julian. But never, not once, had I returned home or had to look Grace in the eye again. Viktor had kept that promise to me.

As of two days ago, I'd returned to start my senior year, which meant that college, life, and the world lay before me. It was a good feeling—one of many I'd come to know here that I never could have experienced back east.

My dorm room might not feel like home, exactly, but I didn't have a home anymore. This campus was as good as anyplace else.

The door to my room opened, and Connor poked his head in. "Dane. You've got mail."

Pushing my chair back from my desk, I raised an eyebrow at my roommate. Mail? Already? I had a feeling I knew what it was, but I was surprised it had arrived so early. I hadn't even been in town a week, after a long, happy summer at Lake Tahoe with friends. "Anything good?"

"Well, my mom didn't send *you* any brownies, so I guess not." Connor tossed the envelope at me ninja-star-style, clutching the small box of aforementioned brownies in his other hand.

I caught the envelope effortlessly and smirked. "Yeah, but those pics she texted me last night sure made up for it."

"You're a funny guy, Dane. Sleep with one eye open tonight." We both laughed as Connor disappeared back out the door.

I called after him, "Seriously, dude, you're not gonna give me one?"

My phone pinged with a text alert, and I set the letter on my desk. When I pulled my phone from my pocket, I thought it was strange that the sender was listed simply as Unknown. As I read the message, the beginnings of a headache tapped at the base of my skull, in perfect concert with every syllable of the words on the screen.

Grace is stealing your father's work. And you're not even here to stop her.

I considered not responding, or even just deleting the text. But curiosity got the better of me. I typed in a short reply with my thumbs and hit send. Who is this?

A friend. A pause, followed by a second text. I'm at the Wills Institute.

Heat crawled up the sides of my neck, hinting at touching my face. What's your name?

The response was immediate. Not important. But what is important is that your sister is finishing your father's work and plans to take all the credit for it.

I rolled my eyes in irritation. I didn't have time for this. You're full of it. And I don't appreciate your little prank. Don't contact me again.

The three dots appeared, signaling that the texter was typing something. Hate it as I did, I couldn't deny my curiosity. I wasn't sure what bothered me more—the fact that the person kept texting me, or the fact that I wanted to know what else they had to say. Finally, the words came through on my screen. I've been watching her. She's crafty. I think she'd do just about anything to have the spotlight all to herself. Don't you?

I did. But that didn't mean I was going to share my feelings with a total stranger . . . or maybe even Grace herself, hiding behind the anonymity of a text message.

The phone pinged again. Maybe even kill for it.

I stared at the message, my head aching, my heart suddenly thumping inside my chest. I whispered aloud, "What do you mean by that exactly?"

I sat there in my chair awhile, breathing in and out, trying to see clearly through the whirlwind of thoughts that had filled my mind. I sent another message. **Who are you?**

I waited, watching the clock. After five full minutes, there was no response. I sent another. **Hello?**

But whoever it was, they were done playing with me for now. They'd stirred up the kind of anxious thoughts that had kept me company for as long as I could remember, only to disappear once again.

Listen, pal. Unless you want to give me some real information, I don't want to hear a word you have to say. So next time you feel like texting me, either include your name with the message or piss off.

I set my phone on the desk and picked up the envelope Connor had brought me. The addresses on the front were in neat handwriting, on lines so straight that it looked as if they'd been written with the aid of a ruler. It was the handwriting of an orderly person, and despite the almost feminine curve to some of the letters, the writer was a man. Not just any man. Viktor.

Once a month, my guardian, my godfather, sent a handwritten letter, sometimes with photos, catching me up on everything he thought I was missing out on. Viktor didn't use a cell phone. He didn't text or Instagram or anything that normal people did. He was one of that strange, rare breed who seemed convinced that the advancement of technology was actually contributing to the decline of polite society . . . or some such crap. He was probably solely responsible for the continued operations of the United States Postal Service. Each letter contained an update on Grace, and gently pleaded with me to consider returning to the Wills Institute. The photographs were never of my sister, just of things that were supposed to remind me of home, and Viktor only dared a sentence or two concerning her well-being and latest accomplishments. Even Viktor, who could be annoyingly persistent when the mood caught him, knew better than to push Grace on me—or the other way around. My sister and I wanted nothing to do with each other. That much was made clear on the day I'd left the Wills Institute to move to California and Grace hadn't even come to say good-bye.

I picked up my phone and scrolled back through the text conversation. Who had sent them? The number was marked as Unknown. It could have been anyone, although they'd acted like they'd known me personally. And had insinuated such ugly things about Grace. Not that I thought my sister wasn't fully capable of stealing our father's research, if she had the motivation. But would she kill for it? Was Grace capable of that kind of evil?

I wished I was certain one way or another. I couldn't help remembering when we were kids and Grace had gotten a new bike for Christmas. Emily from down the street had received the same bike. Only hers was purple, Grace's favorite color, with fancy tassels on the handlebars. Grace was so mad that Emily's bike was better than hers that she tossed Emily's in a Dumpster and watched as the garbage truck crushed it. I saw the whole thing. Only no one believed me.

Grace never touched her pink bike again. She just left it outside beside the garage to rust.

I set the phone down again and ripped open the envelope. Better just to get it over with—read whatever it was that Viktor had to say. A letter, handwritten on vellum, slipped out and into my palm, weighted by something that was folded within. When I saw what it was, my breath caught in my throat. I recognized it instantly.

It was a silver coin from Croatia, marking the 150th anniversary of the birth of Nikola Tesla. One side—the side opposite the image of Tesla's face—had been worn almost bare. It was the coin that my father had always carried with him, the worry stone he'd fiddled with whenever he was trying to work out some detail, some problem that was standing in his way. I had assumed the coin was lost in the fire. And yet here it was, in the palm of my hand.

I unfolded the letter and began to read.

Dearest Adrien,
I hope this letter finds you well.

It does, Viktor. Thank you.

My most recent conversation with your headmaster
told me that your second semester grades were much
improved from the first. I was happy to hear that,
though I would urge you, of course, to really push yourself.
As it is your senior year, it's time to buckle down and
show the world what you've got inside that head of yours.

Blah, blah, blah. Grades aren't everything, Viktor.

He also mentioned that you've even begun participating
in extracurricular activities. Your parents would have
been proud—and I'm sure they are even now, wherever
their souls might rest. Grace sends her regards.

I'm sure she does. I'm sure that's not at all some nicety
you're inserting here just for show.

As usual, she has been excelling academically. She was
named captain of the debate team for her senior year.
I'm sure she misses you very much. It would be nice if
you could extend an olive branch in the form of a letter
or phone call. I fear the space between you both will
only grow wider if one of you doesn't act as the bigger
person and begin the healing process.

Some wounds can't heal, Viktor.

But that's not why I've written to you today.
   Enclosed you'll find your father's coin. I'm sure you
understand the significance of this item, and I thought
that you would greatly appreciate it.

And I do.

It was the strangest thing. I thought for certain
that the coin had melted in the lab fire, but the other
day, as I was tidying up some of the files given to me
by Mr. Sheldon, your parents' lawyer, I found the coin
in the bottom of one of the file boxes. I can only guess
that your father dropped it inside without realizing.
I hope this is a happy accident for you and gives you

something solid to hold on to as you reminisce about what a brilliant, compassionate, trustworthy man your father was.

It means a lot. Thank you.

It was good to see it, to hold it in my hand. It somehow brought Allen closer to me just by touching it, so I hope the coin has the same effect on you. The coin, of course, is yours for the keeping—just as your mother's locket now belongs to Grace.

I realize that your senior year classes will begin on Monday, Adrien, but I implore you. Transfer back to the Wills Institute.

Not a chance, but thanks for asking.

Spend this final year before college in the same school as your sister. It would do this old man's heart good to see you at least attempting a relationship with her. I'm sure that your parents would have wanted better than this for the both of you. Once college begins, I fear that the space between you will grow into a chasm.

It already has.

Please call me after you consider this, so that we can discuss it. I have further information that may affect your thoughts on the matter.

Not likely.

I would have called you with that information first, but I wanted you to have your father's coin in your hand when we speak.

Wait. What?

Take care, Adrien. Of yourself and your sister.
Fondly,
Viktor

I dropped the unfolded letter on my desk and leaned back in my chair, my father's coin cupped in my left palm. I squeezed my eyes shut for a moment, gathering myself. It could only be bad news. Viktor almost never asked me to call.

With a deep breath locked inside my lungs, I punched in the code to unlock my cell phone and pulled up Viktor's landline. By the time I put the phone to my ear, it was already ringing. A feeling of dread had crept into my chest, but I wasn't certain why. Absentmindedly, I began to rub the coin with my other hand.

That familiar, warm, confident voice came over the cell. "Viktor Cadswell speaking. How can I help you?"

"Viktor. It's Adrien."

"Adrien, my boy. How are you? How are things on the sunny West Coast?" Viktor sounded pleasant. Almost too pleasant, like he was laying it on thick.

"Good. Things are good." I glanced at the pages of his letter on my desk and wet my lips before saying, "I just got your letter. You said to call?"

"Of course." Viktor cleared his throat. Maybe he was buying time. Maybe it was nothing. "I want you to know how very much I dread having to tell you this over the phone, Adrien. But it seems there's no other way at the present time. Do you have your father's coin?"

Suddenly, what was left of the air inside my lungs felt heavy and thick, like a fog. "Yeah, it's right here."

"It always helped him in times of stress. I'm hoping it will help you, too, when I share this news with you."

I squeezed the coin between my thumb and forefinger. "Viktor, what is going on?"

There was a pause—one that seemed to stretch out over the afternoon like a large, unexpected cloud on an otherwise sunny day. "Well, I suppose there's no easy way to say this. Months ago, I was diagnosed with pancreatic cancer. I didn't want to worry you or your sister at the time, but now the doctors say that it's advanced to the point where it is inoperable and otherwise untreatable."

"Viktor . . ." I sat up straight in my chair and listened to my breathing for a bit before speaking again. In. Out. In. "Are you saying you're dying?"

The words had left my mouth, but they didn't feel real. Viktor couldn't be dying. There had already been enough death in my life. Enough pain. Enough loss. It had to be some kind of misunderstanding.

Viktor's tone was still warm and kind, but suddenly he sounded like an echo of the man I had always known. "We're all dying, my boy. It's just that my time seems to be growing shorter than several others', yes."

"I don't know what to say. I'm . . . I'm so sorry." The final word cracked as it left my lips.

"Say you'll come home, Adrien. I have maybe six months, perhaps a year on the outside. Come back to Wills. Let me spend time with you and Grace before my time is cut irrevocably short." He was serious, but so calm. So eerily calm. How long had he known that he was dying? Clearly long enough to come to terms with it. Did he hurt? As he sat there, thousands of miles away on the other end of the phone call, was he in pain? Was he suffering? Were there pills in labeled bottles all over his nightstand? Tubes in his nose and arms? Nurses watching him day and night? Why hadn't he told me sooner?

"When am I supposed to come home? I mean, I want to see you, but—"

"There's a red-eye flight that leaves at eleven tonight. If you think you can make it to the airport in time, we can send for the rest of your belongings later. I'll speak to both headmasters this afternoon. I will sort out all the details. Just come home. For Grace. For me."

There was no way. I loved Viktor, but I couldn't face Grace again. Not right now, and definitely not for an entire year. He was asking too much. A few weeks, maybe a month, tops. That was all I could handle—if I could handle that. I knew I was being selfish. Viktor was dying, and I was fretting over seeing my sister. But I'd built a life in California—one I didn't want to leave.

My eyes welled with tears that I refused to let fall. Swallowing them down, I said, "For you, Viktor. Not for Grace. But I want to get back here as soon as I can. It's important."

In true Viktor fashion, he didn't argue. He merely said, "Thank you, Adrien. I'll see you tomorrow."

"Tomorrow. See you then." Hitting the button on my phone to end the call, I put my head back and closed my eyes. Viktor was dying. The closest thing I had left to a father figure—the man who'd stepped in to care for Grace and me when we needed it—was dying.

I looked down at my phone. That's when I realized—I'd been so blindsided by Viktor's news that I'd forgotten about the texts. And now, not ten minutes after an unknown number had begged me to return to Wills, I would, in fact, be returning to Wills. What kind of messed-up coincidence was this?

The door opened once more and Connor stepped inside. The box he'd been holding before was now open, and half the brownies were already missing. When he caught sight of me, he said, "Dude. You look like your dog just died. What's up?"

At this, I stood, grabbed my old military surplus duffel from the closet, and began cramming clothes inside it. "I'm going back east. Just for a month or so. I have some family stuff to deal with."

Connor's jaw dropped. "What? When?"

As I packed, I made sure not to make eye contact with Connor. We'd been best friends since my second year here. It would be hard to leave him. But it was important. "Tonight. I have to. I have no choice."

Connor dropped the box of brownies on my desk in frustration. "You could have warned me sooner that I was going to need a new roommate this year."

I grabbed my cell phone charger and shoved it in the bag. "I'll be back in a month. We're walking down that aisle with polyester dresses and cardboard hats together, dude. Don't worry about it."

But even as I told Connor not to worry, the fear that my plans would get derailed increased. One month. Long enough to say goodbye to Viktor—and to say good-bye to Grace for the rest of our lives. I hated to admit it, but there was a small part of me that was looking forward to the day when Grace and I would no longer have to pretend we were family.

Way too early the next morning, I walked out of security at the airport and pulled the buds from my ears, disconnecting from the mellow sound of a band called Blur. Viktor himself was standing there waiting for me. He was dressed in a three-piece navy suit and polished black shoes. No tubes. Nothing remotely sick-looking about him. The only difference in his appearance from when he'd come to visit last year was the slight hint of gray hair at his temples. He smiled as I approached. I nodded, unable to bend my lips in a way that would seem even remotely happy, and not just because I was totally exhausted. "Viktor."

"Adrien." He placed his hands on my shoulders and squeezed, his smile brightening. "It does my heart so good to see you again. I trust your flight was pleasant enough?"

"Yeah. I slept through most of it."

I looked around, trying to keep my movements cool and casual, even though inside I was feeling anything but. My heart wasn't beating so much as vibrating in my chest because of my nerves. "Is Grace here?"

The truth was, I was feeling more than a little uneasy at the idea of seeing my adoptive sister again. We hadn't laid eyes on each other since the day I'd left for California, and I didn't really feel like I had changed all that much in four years. I was older now, yes. Taller, certainly. But now that I was here, the emotional shards that made up my being were still just as jagged and sharp as they had always been.

Over the years, Viktor had kept me apprised of Grace's life. She was a shoo-in for valedictorian, had many friends, was in many clubs, and on and on and on. She was everything I wasn't, and things had been so much better when we were apart. I didn't know if Grace felt the same way, but it seemed like it. She hadn't texted or called me even once in four years. Seemed like a mutual feeling to me.

Viktor took a moment before responding, as if gathering his words carefully. "She's sleeping in. She thought you might want some time to talk with me before you saw her."

I sighed, running a hand through my tousled hair. "Right. Which means you thought you should see me first so you could lecture me on getting along with her."

"Your sister isn't exactly the uncaring monster you make her out to be."

But Viktor didn't know Grace like I did. She was very good at putting up a front when the right people were looking. The girl could have won an Oscar for her acting, if only it were on-screen instead of in her everyday life.

"Please. Grace only cares about Grace, Viktor. Always has. Always will."

A silence hung between us—one full of both understanding and disagreement. The calm, patient smile had left Viktor's face. "Do you have any more luggage to collect?"

I held up my duffel bag by the straps. "This is all I brought."

Viktor nodded, and when he turned toward the glass doors, I followed. The awkwardness between us was unbearable, and I knew it was mostly my fault it was there. Viktor was very much a keep-the-peace kind of person, whereas I didn't give a crap about rocking the boat. Better to speak the truth and upset someone than lie your way through life with a smile on your face. But still . . . I hated hurting Viktor.

As we stepped outside and crossed the street to the parking garage, I cleared my throat and said, "How are you feeling, anyway?"

Viktor withdrew his key fob from his pocket and pressed the unlock button on his silver Lexus. As he opened the driver's side door, he said, "Tired, I suppose. But I'd wager that most of my weariness is from preparations for the new school year. I'm in no more pain than I usually am. To tell the truth, I don't feel sick. Not really. Does that surprise you?"

"Honestly, yes." I opened the passenger's side door and tossed my bag in the backseat. "I half expected to see you attached to an oxygen tank."

Laughter escaped Viktor, and he slid into the driver's seat. I joined him inside the car, relieved to hear him laugh. He said, "It's a good thing you're not going into the medical field, my boy. It's not always like you see in the movies. I swear to you, I feel quite fine, apart from a little underslept."

I wasn't sure whether this was entirely a good thing. It was honestly a little scarier that his illness bore no visible signs—that he could hardly feel it. Part of me worried that Viktor might drop dead right in front of me at any second.

I spent the drive back to Viktor's house staring out the windows. Every once in a while, on either side of the road, there was a break in the trees. Sometimes the break held a house, sometimes an old barn or other abandoned building. There were only a few other cars and trucks on the road. I'd almost forgotten what it looked like out here.

"How is Julian handling the news that you're sick?"

"He doesn't know. And I intend to keep it that way for as long as possible." A semitruck passed us on the left, its engine roaring. Viktor's sunglasses may have been able to hide his eyes, but they couldn't hide the tension in his jaw.

Julian and Viktor had been together since Grace and I were in kindergarten. Julian felt as much a part of my family as Viktor did. "Don't you think that's a bit . . . I dunno . . . cruel? Not to tell him that he's losing you?"

After an uncomfortably long beat, Viktor spoke at last, his words soft but certain. "If you'd known you were going to lose your parents, but had no idea what day it would happen, wouldn't that have been a larger burden than just having it happen suddenly? I don't want to draw out his pain."

My chest felt heavy at the mention of my parents, but I understood why Viktor had brought them up. Even if I did disagree with not telling Julian about his illness. "He loves you, Viktor. You shouldn't lie to him. Especially not about this. And withholding information is the same as lying."

Viktor's left hand moved slightly, pressing the blinker lever down. He turned and drove through the black iron gates at the front of his home. "Why don't we agree that I will leave the topic of you and your sister alone, so long as you leave my business with Julian and my illness alone?"

I mumbled a halfhearted but affirmative response.

I had always loved visiting Viktor when my parents were alive. He had one of the most beautiful homes I had ever seen. In the years that I'd been away, I'd forgotten just how beautiful.

The house sat at the end of a long, gravel driveway with a circle in front. Not at all like the gravel you might find on a dirt road in the country, but polished, white river rock. The grounds were well groomed, with flower beds placed throughout. Julian had quite the green thumb, I remembered now. My mom had often commented on how jealous she was about that. As a botanist, she felt like she should have the prettier garden, but Julian refused to let her. It had been a playful argument between them for years.

Viktor and Julian's two-story redbrick home was huge— far bigger than two men alone required. But, as Viktor liked to brag, it was on the national registry of historic homes, and I think that's what appealed to him most. It had been built in the seventeen hundreds and was used as a hospital during the Revolutionary War. As we approached the end of the drive, I could see Julian coming out the front door. The look in his eyes was happy, eager. It hurt to know that he'd lose his husband soon and had no idea it was coming.

"I still think you should tell him," I said.

The car came to a stop in front of the house. Julian

opened his arms in greeting, a smile on his lips. I reached for the door handle, but was halted by Viktor's hand on my shoulder.

"You should know that I asked Grace to join us for dinner tonight." He was facing me now that the car had stopped. And the look in his eyes was almost pleading. Pleading with me to play nice with my sister. The one thing that I did not think it was possible to do.

"Awesome." I resisted the urge to roll my eyes, reminding myself that I was doing this for him.

"Adrien. You've gotten so tall." As I stepped out of the car, Julian hugged me and then held me back by the shoulders, looking me over. "And still so resistant to the idea of ironing. I guess an overnight flight is a good excuse, at least."

I forced a smile at his jab. Despite his criticism, I'd always liked Julian. Ever since Viktor had begun inviting him to dinner parties at my parents' home, back when Viktor was still pretending that they were just colleagues and nothing more. It was Julian who'd shared their happy news when they became engaged, and everyone we knew accepted it with a smile. Who could fault them for finding happiness?

"It's good to see you, Julian. How've you been?"

"Wonderful. Viktor may have already mentioned it,

but I've accepted a teaching position at Wills, starting this year. Mostly I'll be teaching freshman English, but I'm also leading one of the new electives they're offering for all years—one that focuses on communication. I'd love to have you in class, but I'm betting you'll be more interested in the forensics elective."

It's true, the word *forensics* grabbed my attention far more than *communication*. But this was Julian's first teaching job in years, and it's not like I would be taking any classes here for longer than a month. "Sounds interesting. Maybe I'll sign up for it."

"I hope so. I could use a friendly face in the crowd." He turned and kissed Viktor lightly on the cheek. "How was the drive?"

"Delightfully uneventful." Viktor smiled at Julian, his eyes sparkling. As we walked into the house, Viktor tossed his car keys my way. "Would you mind hanging those up for me?"

"Sure thing." A small wooden cabinet hung on the wall just inside the door, just as it had for years. As I opened the cabinet door, I saw several sets of keys hanging on the hooks inside. I moved my hand from set to set, examining them. On the last hook was a set of keys with a key ring labeled *Maggie*.

My heart skipped a beat as I slipped the key ring off the

hook and held the keys tightly in my hand. Memories of my dad, wearing dirty coveralls and covered in grease, a far cry from the lab coat and glasses that he usually wore, came flooding back to me.

Out of the corner of my eye I saw Viktor watching me. "She's in the garage under a tarp." He smiled. "She needs a new set of tires and a tune-up, but I'm sure she could be ready to go in no time."

Viktor looked pointedly into my eyes. "And of course, now that you're here, she's yours."

His words entered my ears and flew through my body in a cascade of utter joy. Maggie was mine. After all this time.

"Thank you, Viktor. You have no idea what this means to me." Initially, our agreement was that I could have Maggie at the age of sixteen if I remained at Wills, or after graduation if I left. I'd be lying if I said I hadn't already thought about what would happen to her now that I was back only temporarily. I guess I had my answer now. Or at least her keys.

My father's keys. My keys. I put them in my front pocket. Maggie was mine at last. As it should be.

After an epic nap that lasted most of the day, dinner smells called me down to the dining room. Roasted chicken, mashed potatoes, asparagus. It smelled like Julian had made my favorite foods for my first night back.

The pocket doors stood open at the end of the hall, revealing the formal dining room. I stepped inside and took my seat across from my sister.

Grace didn't look all that different than she had four years before. She was older now, of course, but in almost every respect, she still looked like the Grace I remembered. Prim. Proper. Perfect.

She nodded a curt greeting, her eyes sweeping over but not really stopping on me. "Adrien."

"Grace." I nodded back. It was all very formal, all very fake. Like everything between my sister and me.

"You're so much taller than you were."

"Your hair is shorter."

We were pointing out the obvious while we waited for some sort of familiarity to creep in. I doubted that would ever happen. I glanced at Viktor and Julian as they took their seats together at the end of the table, but they were no help. Perhaps they were hoping that five minutes of idle chatter might repair the silence of the past four years. They were wrong. I couldn't bear to tell them how wrong.

Grace smoothed out her napkin on her lap and managed a polite smile. But her words were taunting, as if she was trying to get me to lose my cool. "How's your GPA?"

It had always been this way. Grace was the daughter who could do no wrong, with perfect grades and a blossoming social life. I was the bright son with no real drive to speak of. I had friends, sure . . . most of whom I hung out with in detention. And yet she still insisted on comparing us, as though I was even trying to compete.

I lifted my right shoulder in a shrug, letting her words roll off me. "I'm doing all right. Business as usual."

"Same with me. A four-point-oh, in case you were curious." She adjusted in her seat, as if her posture could get any straighter.

"I wasn't." The air grew warm, then heavy, then silent.

The grandfather clock in the hall was ticking loudly as the seconds passed. Finally, Julian cleared his throat and said, "Why don't we all have a drink before dinner?"

"I don't drink." I'd had a drink or three, sure. But I didn't care much for it. In my experience, drinking only led to headaches—both the figurative and literal kind.

"I wasn't offering you alcohol, Adrien." Julian pasted on that Julian smile, probably hoping to lighten the air a bit.

"I'll make some herbal tea." Grace began to stand, but Viktor shook his head and gestured for her to remain seated.

"Don't be silly. You and Adrien sit here and catch up while Julian and I finish getting everything ready." Viktor stood from his chair and motioned for Julian to join him.

"I'll be back in a minute with some tea. And a Mountain Dew for you, Adrien?" He grabbed Julian's arm, and they exited the room. As proper as Viktor usually acted, it was practically a shove out the door.

"Well." Grace folded her napkin again and set it on the table. It was as if she needed to move around in order to maintain calm. Chaos to control. She lowered her voice, as if we were sharing some kind of secret. "This is awkward."

No secret there. Grace hadn't gotten any worse at pointing out the obvious. "It usually is when two strangers are left in a room to shoot the shit."

"Honestly." She was visibly disturbed by my choice of words. "We're hardly strangers."

"Oh really?" I raised a defiant eyebrow. "What's my favorite color?"

She opened her mouth to speak, but changed her mind and pursed her lips. I reveled a little in being right. There was something oddly satisfying about annoying my sister.

"Y'know, you didn't have to run away from everyone and leave Wills." She continued not to look at me when she spoke.

I looked at my silverware. The low light of the chandelier was reflected in the shiny surfaces. I wondered how long Viktor and Julian planned to keep up this torture. "But you're glad I did?"

I wasn't sure why it had left my mouth as a question. I already knew the answer, and honestly couldn't give a crap about it.

"I'd be lying if I said I haven't enjoyed these last four years with you being gone. Your absence has certainly eased the tension around here."

"Well, I won't be here for long, so you can go ahead and get on with life as usual, Your Highness."

She didn't respond. Merely sipped from her water glass. For some reason, that got under my skin worse than anything.

"So basically you think I'm back to screw up your picture-perfect life. Is that what you're saying?" I knew I was egging her on. I didn't care. It had been too long and too much had remained unsaid.

"I never said that. But then again, I don't suppose I had to. Did I?" The napkin went back in her lap again. I wished she would make up her mind about where she wanted it. I was tired of watching her fidget.

"I wasn't the only one who caused problems between us, Grace."

"No, but you started them." Finally, she met my eyes. It was the first time she had really looked at me since our parents had died. "Probably out of your relentless need for attention."

"Don't tell me—you took a psych class last semester, didn't you?" I rolled my eyes. "You're not going to start analyzing me now, are you?"

"Of course not. I just think we should settle some things before classes begin." The napkin was back on the table.

"Fine. Let's do that, then." I dropped my napkin on the table, too. While hers was neatly folded, mine was in a heap on my plate. I was done pretending to be nice, not that either of us were doing a very good job at that. "Why did you take those pages from Dad's journal?"

Grace sighed with an air of impatience. "Adrien. That was four years ago."

"It may as well have been yesterday for me." She averted her eyes again. I wasn't sure if it was from shame, or if she just hated me so much that she couldn't stand to look at me. "I received a text from someone yesterday morning who said you were planning to take credit for Dad's work. Is it true?"

"Who sent it?"

I could tell that my voice was beginning to rise. If Viktor and Julian couldn't hear me by now, they would soon. "Who sent the text isn't important. Is it true or isn't it?"

"You're being ridiculous."

"That's not denial."

"It's also not confirmation."

Viktor entered the dining room carrying drinks. Julian was right behind him, a bowl of mashed potatoes in his hands. "Herbal tea for you, Grace. And a Mountain Dew for you, Adrien. Would you like a glass? With ice, perhaps?"

"No, thanks." I popped open the tab on the can and took a long swig. "Grace and I were just discussing honesty and integrity. Two qualities she apparently oozes from her pores."

Grace picked up the teacup in her hands, blowing the steam from the top. After she took a sip, she returned the cup to its saucer and said, "I can't recall. Do you have any siblings, Julian?"

"Four. One brother, three sisters. I'm the middle child."

She touched the edges of her lips with her napkin. "Are you close?"

"Very. We had the usual fights when we were younger, but once we all got out of high school and into college, things settled down between us." He sighed as he retook his seat at the end of the table. "I wouldn't say we're the best of friends, but we're definitely close. Holiday visits, phone calls. You know."

"I wish I had a sibling I could talk to." Her voice was breathy with sadness, longing. It made me sick to hear it. Sick . . . and furious.

"Bullshit." I flashed a glare at her. "Let's face it, Grace. You never wanted me in your life. Not from day one. Don't pretend you ever did."

"I said a sibling. Not an orphan that we took in out of pity." That dig was a little harsh, even for Grace, and I'd be lying if I said it didn't sting a little.

"And you say she's not a terrible person." I muttered my words to Viktor, who'd grown rather quiet since he returned to the dining room carrying trays of food.

"This smells great." Julian was making an obvious attempt to quell the tension in the room. His attempt was obviously failing. "Nice to have a few last home-cooked meals before you eat three times a day in the dining hall, eh?"

I thought I'd humor him with a response. "Wills does have kitchens we can use in the dorms. But other than late-night cookie baking, I doubt I'll use it."

"What about you, Grace?" The sweetness in his voice was way over the top.

"Hmm?"

Julian forced a smile. "Do you miss home-cooked meals during the school year?"

Grace seemed distracted. She poked a piece of chicken with a tine of her fork before jabbing it and placing it on her plate. "It's wonderful, thank you."

"Enough of this." Viktor dropped his fork and knife on his plate with a loud clang.

"Viktor." Julian stretched his arm out, catching Viktor's hand in his. The eternal peacemaker, more so even than Viktor. "I don't think now is the time."

"There couldn't be a better time. And I refuse to eat

another bite until we get this settled." Viktor wiped his mouth on his blue linen napkin and returned it to his lap. When he regarded us with his eyes, it was clear that he meant business. "Adrien. Grace. You clearly have problems between you. I've been gentle, understanding, and patient. But I have reached the end of my ability to sit back and wait for you to communicate with each other. I tire of the constant needling, the underhanded insults. We are not leaving this table until you two say whatever it is that you feel needs to be said. Who wants to go first?"

I glanced at Grace. What was this?

By the look on Grace's face, she had no idea.

"Fine. We'll do this alphabetically then." Viktor leaned forward and nodded to me. "Adrien, tell your sister why you carry so much venom for her."

Why? Why was easy. But I wasn't entirely convinced that Viktor wanted to hear it. "What do you want me to say exactly?"

"You call her vile names and glare every time she enters the room. I think she deserves to know why. Out with it."

"Because she—"

"To her." Viktor pointed to Grace.

I took a breath and drummed my fingers absentmindedly for a moment on the table before looking at Grace. Once I did, the words came out of me in an honest puff.

"Since I can remember, you've acted like I'm not a member of the Dane family. You've always treated me like some kind of charity case. I call you a terrible person . . . because you're a terrible person. Also because I try not to use the word *bitch* when I can help it."

My words didn't even make her flinch. Maybe she was used to being called a bitch. Maybe worse. She pursed her lips and looked me in the eye. "Maybe I'm a bitch to you because of the way you treat me. Did you ever think of that? You say horrible things about me every time I see you—"

"Because of the way you act toward me."

"—and you act as if Mom and Dad treated me like some pampered princess, when we were always treated like equals." In a huff, she picked up her fork and stabbed at her potatoes. "Despite the fact that we shouldn't have been."

"And we come to the center of the shrubbery maze!" I laughed, but it wasn't natural. I was angry and feeling more than a little bit bitter. "How do you think I should have been treated? Like some kind of long-term houseguest?"

"Like their *adopted* son." She picked up her napkin and held it to the corner of her eye. It was a ploy for sympathy that she had used in the past, but there were no tears there. Not even the threat of tears. "Not like their *actual* son."

Julian opened his mouth to intervene, but Viktor held up a hand to stop him.

"For all intents and purposes, I *am* their actual son. They're listed on my birth certificate as my parents."

"That was changed as part of the adoption procedure. Genetically, you're no more connected to them than a housecat."

"You know what your problem is, Grace?"

She returned her napkin to her lap and regained her immaculate posture. "Please. Enlighten me."

"They *chose* me." The venom in my voice was thick. Thick and intentional. "They got stuck with you."

Grace's cheeks were flushed, her eyes sharp, her lips tight. Maybe she thought that I'd gone too far. Oh, but there was so much further I could go.

The room was silent for several moments. Viktor finally broke in. "Are you two finished? Is there anything more that you need to say to each other to lay all this negativity to rest?"

I looked at Grace pointedly. "When did you steal the pages from Dad's notebook? Exactly when?"

She met my gaze with daggers. "The day we had that horrible professional picture taken."

There was only one more thing that I needed to know. "Can I see what's on them?"

"No."

"Why?"

Grace spoke clearly, putting emphasis on each word, as

if they were separate sentences. "Because they belong in the family. And you are definitely not family."

I stood up, pushing my chair back. As I left the room, Viktor called after me, "Adrien, where are you going?"

I stopped in my tracks just outside the pocket doors. "Excuse me, Viktor. Julian. It would seem I've lost my appetite."

[CHAPTER 3]

ACIDIC SOLUTION:

Any solution that has a higher concentration of hydrogen ions than water does

I found my appetite the next morning when the smell of bacon and eggs wafted its way up the stairs to my room. I lay there, staring up at the painting of a young girl wearing a gas mask that hung on the wall beside my bed. This room had always been mine, just as Grace's room here had always been hers. Sleeping over at Viktor's house had been a normal part of our lives for as long as I could remember. Still . . . it felt weird being back here, for some reason.

Throwing on a T-shirt and jeans over the boxers I'd slept in, I made my way down the stairs to the breakfast nook. Julian was standing at the stove in a burgundy terry cloth robe, humming as he poured pancake batter into a pan. I took a seat at the table and he greeted me with a smile, his blue eyes twinkling. "Hungry? I made plenty."

My stomach rumbled an answer. I hadn't eaten since lunch the day before—the price of my righteous indignation last night. When Julian pushed a plate across the counter to me, I stood to retrieve it and sat back down, immediately shoveling a forkful of scrambled eggs into my mouth.

"Where's Viktor this morning? Won't he be joining us?" I didn't ask about my sister. Mostly because I didn't care. In fact, I had a few good ideas on where she could go.

"He and Grace drove over to Wills to get a few things in order before classes start on Monday. I can drive you over and help get you settled after we do a little shopping. It'll take a few days to get your belongings all shipped over from California, so we should buy you enough to get your school year started." He flipped a pancake over and turned to look at me. "Do you want to talk about last night?"

Through a mouthful of eggs, I said, "I don't need my stuff shipped in. I don't know what Viktor told you, but I'm only staying a month. And as for last night, I'd rather not talk about it. But something tells me I don't have much choice in the matter."

Julian quietly moved a finished pancake onto his plate, turned off the stove, and filled the rest of his plate with bacon and eggs. As he sat down beside me, I swallowed a mouthful of crisp bacon and said, "Let me see if I can sum it up and save you the energy. I should be nicer to my sister, because she's really a very sweet, gentle person who needs me now more than ever, blah, blah, blah. . . . Am I close?"

He picked up his fork and met my eyes. "Actually, I was going to say that she said some horrible things to you last night, and if that's the way things normally are between you, I can't blame you for never wanting to see her."

I took another bite of bacon and chewed it slowly, wondering if this was some kind of sarcastic joke or something. I said, "Wow, Julian. You're not like Viktor. He would have said the exact opposite."

"Well, you know what they say, opposites attract." We continued to eat our breakfast in comfortable silence. It was nice to know that Julian understood my feelings, at least partially. "So listen, Adrien—I'm confused. Viktor said that you'd be graduating from Wills."

I set my fork down, the metal clanking against the porcelain. It sounded much louder than I'd intended. "Well, he's wrong. I only came back here to . . . deal with some personal stuff, and then I'm going right back to my school. I don't know what to do about Viktor. It's like he's asking me for the one thing I can't ever give him. He wants me to do something about my relationship with Grace. To fix it or something. I keep telling him I don't have a relationship with her and don't want one. I've never had a relationship with Grace. So why start now?"

"He just wants peace. It makes sense, considering his condition." He met my eyes, and I could see the knowledge of Viktor's disease written all over his face.

Still, I had promised my godfather that I wouldn't say anything. No matter how ridiculous I thought the notion was. "Condition?"

Julian reached over and cupped my hand, giving it a squeeze. "It's all right, Adrien. I know all about Viktor's health problems. He may think he's capable of hiding a terminal illness from me, but he's mistaken. I may be younger than him, but I'm not an idiot. I know he's . . . I know he's dying."

"He asked me not to say anything. I'm so sorry, Julian."

"Thank you." He gave my hand another squeeze and picked his fork up again, moving the eggs around on his plate before speaking. "And thank you for honoring his wishes."

It looked as if it was his turn to lose his appetite. Who could blame him? He and Viktor had been together for going on thirteen years. They shared a life.

But in true Julian fashion, he forced a smile. "I look at it like this. There are two ways that I can approach losing him. One, I can throw myself into the emotional abyss and wrap myself in a cocoon of mourning. Or two, I can say 'screw it all' and get on with things, squeezing every drop of joy that I can out of our remaining days together. I choose the latter."

I thought about how it had felt to sit in the headmaster's office and learn that I'd never see my parents again. Even now, there was no grave to visit, no private place where I could commune with my memories of them. There were just cold metal urns filled with even colder ashes, sitting atop a fireplace mantel in a room I'd spent the last twenty-four hours avoiding at all costs.

I felt like I should offer him some solace, some shred of hope. But all I had to go on was my experience. "I'm still mourning my parents. It takes time, y'know. There's no set calendar for things like this. And who knows, maybe the doctors will turn out to be quacks who gave him the wrong time frame. It happens sometimes. We don't have to mourn him just yet."

"You were only a boy when you lost them. Hardly ready to be thrust into the world on your own. I can't even imagine how difficult it's been for you." The air around us had changed. I shifted in my seat a little. "But as harsh as it may sound . . . sooner or later, Adrien, you're going to have to look forward instead of back. We all do."

"Now you do sound like Viktor." I stood from my chair, grabbed a glass from the counter, and poured myself some juice.

"What can I say? He brings out the best in me." A smile crossed Julian's lips as he winked at me. The love and respect that he had for Viktor was undeniable. It was free, easy, obvious.

"Grace brings out the worst in me."

I had a specific incident in mind when I said this, though it was one I hadn't thought about in years. Grace and I were standing in the backyard of our house—just kids, maybe nine or ten years old. We were standing in our mom's garden. Not the greenhouse, never there. We weren't allowed. Mom had told us countless times that her greenhouse was for cross-pollination experiments and interspecies plant breeding. It was her place—a place for her work. Not even Dad was allowed in there.

We were outside, in her personal garden, where Mom spent her mornings relaxing with her plants rather than cataloging and studying them. It was a peaceful place for her, and she referred to the time she spent every morning tending to each bloom as her "Zen time."

Grace and I were arguing, which already by then wasn't out of the ordinary for us. Only this time we were arguing over a species of a particular plant in the garden. The flower in question was lovely and white with purple accents on the petals. Grace insisted it was an *Orchidaceae dendrobium*, a genus of orchid commonly referred to as a "King's Jewel Pink Crystal." But she was wrong. While it was an orchid, it was the more uncommon Minho Princess "Water Color Artist." I knew, because Mom had told me the day before.

When I pointed out her error, making note that the purple veined its way through, rather than just appearing as spots on the petals, Grace set her jaw and ignored me. I raised my voice so she'd have no choice but to listen, but she plugged her ears and started humming this annoying song by John Mayer that she knew I hated. The heat of anger burned through my veins. She couldn't just listen to reason, to me. She'd rather shut me out than admit that she was wrong. Before I realized what I was doing, I had picked her up by the throat and screamed into her frightened face.

I'm not a violent person. I never have been. I'd much rather talk my way out of a disagreement than fight my way out. But on that day, with Grace's smug little face in front of me humming that irritating song, all I wanted to do was shut her up and make her listen, by whatever means I could.

I was wrong to do it. I had known it then. I still knew it now.

I never touched her again, either, though there'd been

plenty of times when I'd felt the same urge to shut her up for a moment and make her listen.

"And you bring out the worst in her." Julian raised his eyebrows as he looked up from his plate. "I remember your dad always used to describe you two with a chemistry analogy. He said you can have two different substances that, by themselves, operate in wonderful ways. But when combined, they're volatile. Maybe even explosive, if you're not careful. And I think it's true—that's you and Grace. You're both wonderful people who prove absolutely volatile whenever you're around each other. You have to learn how to handle your interactions with the greatest of delicacy."

The phone on the wall rang, interrupting our breakfast life lesson. Julian set his fork down on the table and picked up the receiver. I only partially paid attention to the half of the conversation that I could hear. From the tone of Julian's voice and the things that he was saying, it was obvious that my godfather was on the other end of the line. I was more interested in another serving of bacon. Julian had been right last night. A good home-cooked meal was a lot better than eating in the cafeteria at school. I folded the bacon into a piece of toast and sank my teeth in just as Julian hung up the phone.

"That was Viktor. He spoke to the headmaster, and they're arranging your room placement and preliminary class schedule as we speak. They're trying to match as many of the classes you had in California as possible." He returned to the table, but rather than sitting down to finish eating, he started clearing the dishes. It was as if hearing from Viktor was our cue to get on with the day. But then, it had always been that way. Viktor had always been in charge. "I know it must be hard, changing schools your senior year. But I can't tell you how much it means to Viktor. In many ways, he views you and your sister as his children. We both do. I think he's just trying to take care of you both, make certain that things are mended between you before his time comes."

And there he went again. I was beginning to think that this was going to be the mantra for my entire stay here. I'd barely been back in town for a full twenty-four hours, and I was already sick of hearing that Grace and I needed to work things out between us. "Look, Julian, it's not like I haven't tried to get along with Grace. And as much as I'd love to give Viktor that beautiful deathbed moment that he's looking for, I just . . ."

Julian dropped a juice glass into the sink, and broken shards exploded against the side. He lifted his hand to his eyes, willing the tears to stay inside. Apparently he wasn't handling the news of Viktor's illness as well as he'd let on. I instantly felt like the biggest ass in the world. "Julian, I'm sorry. I should have chosen my words more carefully."

He was quiet for a long time. His hands were shaking.

"You want my advice? No bullshit? Man to man?" He dropped his trembling hand to the counter and stared out the window above the sink. That moment had been just enough for him to regain his composure. "Fake it."

I swallowed hard, not understanding. "Fake it?"

"Yes, fake it. Play nice until you two go your separate ways. Make your godfather happy. Even if it isn't real." He started picking up the broken pieces of glass, still not willing to look at me. "Do you seriously think that knowing how sick he is and the fact that he doesn't feel the need to share that with me doesn't hurt like hell, Adrien? It does. But I fake it because I love him."

Julian moved across the room and dropped the remnants of the glass into the garbage can. He walked over to me and put his hands on my shoulders. Finally, he met my eyes. "I mean, really, how often are you going to have to pretend for him? When you pass him in the halls at school? When you join us for dinner on the occasional weekend? Christmas break, if you stay that long? When you think about it, is it such a sacrifice to make in order to please a man who cares so dearly for you both? To grant his dying wish?"

He was right, of course. But there were two sides to this coin, and I could only be in control of one of them. "What about Grace?"

A wrinkle settled across Julian's forehead. It was clear that he was just as concerned as I was about the other side of that coin. "I'll talk to her."

"Then I'll try my best." Julian squeezed my shoulder before removing his hands. I could see the *thank you* in his eyes.

"Come on, let's get out of here already. We have some shopping to do."

Shopping with Julian was more fun than it probably should have been. But as we made our way through the linens section to pick out sheets, I found myself smiling. It actually felt good to go through such mundane back-to-school tasks with a parental figure. It had been a long time.

Julian held up two sets of sheets. "Cotton or flannel?"

I shrugged, not really caring all that much. But it was the last thing on our list and apparently it mattered to Julian. I said, "Flannel's softer. More . . . I dunno, inviting."

"Expecting company? Because condoms are in aisle six." Julian waggled his eyebrows and I laughed out loud.

"Next subject, please." My face flushed, but I tried not to act embarrassed. "I have two ties. That's more than enough. But I might need to get the new uniform jackets tailored."

As we headed for the checkout, Julian lowered his voice and gave my sleeve a tug as we passed aisle six. "Just so you know, I wasn't entirely kidding about the condoms. If you need them. No judgment."

A groan escaped my throat, and I rolled my eyes. "Julian."

He held his hands up in defense. "Just checking."

The drive to Wills was relatively short, and we sat in the car in the parking lot of my new dorm for a moment before getting out. A sudden, strange wave of nervousness washed over me. I was pretty sure Julian could tell, but I was grateful that he didn't say anything. "I'll be living in the tower, eh? I thought it was closed."

"They refurbished it last summer. There are only four rooms up there, but they're larger than the main-floor rooms." Julian peered up out of the windshield, straining to see the top of the building. "With closets, even. So no more wardrobe and footlocker to worry about."

I got out of the car. It was much easier to see the top of the tower from here. "Yeah, that's great and all, but it looks like the trade-off is a whole lot of stairs."

"The exercise will be good for your brain." Julian grabbed the shopping bags from the backseat and pushed two of them across the roof to me.

"Yeah, but it'll kill my thighs."

As we walked into the main entrance of the dorm building, the familiar sights and sounds of move-in day flooded my senses. The bustle of people all trying to fit in the doors at once. The high-pitched squeals from friends who hadn't seen one another over the break. The *clackity-clack* of suitcases being pulled along the tile floor. New students and transfer students looking lost as they searched for their rooms. The scene had been the same in California as it was here, although in California we got to move in the full week before classes started. It sort of helped with the traffic, but really move-in day was move-in day everywhere.

Only, I wasn't moving into some random new school somewhere in the country. I was back at the Wills Institute. Back at the place where I'd last lived with my parents. I'd be lying if I said that I hadn't missed it, just a little bit.

When we finally reached the top of the tower stairs, I counted four doors on the floor. Which meant eight people would share the space, two to a room. When I'd left, there had been talk of making the dorms co-ed by room, but I couldn't imagine that had been well received by parents. Wills had a relatively low teen pregnancy rate, and they probably wanted to keep it that way. "All guys up here?"

"Yes. And in case you're curious, Grace is in a room two floors down, all the way on the other side of the building." Julian led me to the farthest door on the left and dangled a key in front of my eyes. "Do you want to do the honors?"

I slid the key in the lock and turned it, twisting the

knob until the door swung open. The room was fairly small. Bare wooden beams crossed the ceiling. The walls were unpainted. It looked more like a storage room than a dorm room. All wood, no color, and just one small window. I raised an eyebrow as I looked around. "Are you sure they renovated it?"

"It's not that bad. Actually, the architecture is quite charming." Julian did have a point. If by "charming" he meant "prisonlike."

"No offense, Julian, but you must annoy the crap out of Viktor with your unfailing optimism in all things."

Julian walked through the door and set the bags on one of the beds. I reluctantly crossed the threshold and made my way into the room. I looked at the two identical beds, two identical dressers, two identical desks, and the small sink between the two identical closet doors. Considering how prisonlike it felt, I was both pleased and surprised not to find a metal toilet in the corner. Still, I had to glance back at the door behind me. I'd half expected to find iron bars blocking the opening.

Julian was happily removing clothes from the shopping bags, folding them, and putting them in one of the dressers. I set the rest of my bags, full of school supplies and toiletries, on the adjacent desk.

"Well then, that'll do for now." Julian surveyed his work with an air of accomplishment. "Why don't we go collect your class schedule?"

Forty-five minutes later, I sat with Julian in the coffee shop just off campus looking over the classes for my senior year. Literature, chemistry, calculus, biology, economics, and . . . communication.

I bit the inside of my cheek, kind of bummed that I hadn't been able to take forensics as well. "Looks like Viktor was able to get me into your class."

"Oh good!" Julian shook a couple of sugar packets before tearing them open and pouring them into his steaming cup. "We'll be spending our afternoons together."

"Yeah." I eyed the classes warily. Not that I found them intimidating. With such a small senior class, there was a fifty-fifty chance that I'd have at least one or two of them with Grace. I couldn't imagine sitting in class with her every day. And I'd be damned if we were going to be lab partners.

Julian sipped his coffee, decided that it was still too hot, and returned the cup to the table. "You know you're welcome to stay with us any time if you get sick of dorm life. No judgment. Just say the word."

"Julian." I placed my hand over his on the table and looked him in the eye. "I've got this."

"I'm just trying to make sure you're happy." He returned my pointed stare. "Are you, Adrien? Have you found happiness on the West Coast? Or whatever it is that you're looking for out there?"

I sat back in my chair and sipped my latte. I wasn't a huge fan of coffee, but a latte was a different story altogether. It was mostly milk and sweetener, with just enough coffee to make me seem mature, but without the bitter, nasty taste of actually drinking coffee. "Happy is a relative term. I'm okay. I keep busy. I laugh. I spend time with other people when the mood strikes me."

"People? Hmm." He raised an eyebrow at me as he took another sip from his cup. "A girlfriend, perhaps?"

"Don't be ridiculous."

"A boyfriend, then?" I gave him a look—not to deny anything, but to ask him to back out of my personal life. He held up his palms defensively. "I just want to know that you're talking to someone when you have a bad day."

Boyfriends. Girlfriends. Aardvarks. Whatever I might be in to, it was my business and mine alone.

"I have friends. We talk sometimes." I took another drink and glanced around the café. For the first time, it really hit me that I had left Connor and all my friends on the other side of the country. And even a month was a long time to be away. Who *would* I talk to here when I had a bad day?

"What do you talk about? Your family? About what happened?" He was looking at me over the rim of his coffee cup in that way that adults do when they want you to know that they're concerned about your well-being. That way that said, *I know I'm prying, but I'm only doing so because I care.*

"No. Never about that." This was just what I needed. It wasn't bad enough that I'd been dragged away from my life in California to spend time with Grace—now he wanted to talk about my dead parents. One of Viktor's conditions of my moving out west was that I'd see a counselor to deal with my grief. I'd gone twice. As far as I was concerned, it had been enough to fulfill my obligation—especially considering I hadn't wanted to go see the guy in the first place. "Why would I talk about that?"

"Because maybe talking about it will ease your pain." I knew that he was only trying to help. I knew that he had the best of intentions. However, this was the one subject that I didn't want to talk about. With anyone. Male. Female. Whatever. As far as I was concerned, the topic was off-limits.

"Julian."

"I know. I know. I'm prying." He returned his cup to the table. "Will you have one more dinner with us before we lose you to dorm life? It would make Viktor happy to have you for another night."

When I hesitated to respond, he said, "Come on. I'll make a pot roast."

It was a tempting offer. Julian did make one hell of a pot roast. But I thought that I might be able to sweeten the deal. "And a cherry crumble?"

A smile settled on his lips. He knew exactly what I was doing. He also knew that Viktor was the whole reason I'd come back from California. There was no way I was going to say no to an evening with the two of them. "Of course."

"When will you discuss things with Grace?" I had a feeling she would be invited to dinner as well, and I wanted to do my best to keep my promise. "Our arrangement?"

"Tonight." Julian's brow dropped. "Are you having second thoughts?"

"No, I just . . ." A tension had settled at the base of my spine. "She may not agree. And then Viktor . . ."

"She'll agree to keep the peace for Viktor's sake, Adrien. You both care about him. There's no reason she won't." He set his cup on the table and met my eyes. "Besides, I'm the one asking her, not you. She'll say yes."

After a quick run to the bookstore, we returned to my dorm room with a new leather messenger bag filled with all the books I'd need for the coming school year. The door swung open, revealing a thin boy in jeans and a short-sleeved plaid shirt. His hair was dirty blond and could have used a comb. He looked surprised to see us, but quickly recovered and smiled. "Hey. I'm Quinn. You must be Adrien."

"Yeah. I guess we're roommates, eh?" I shook the newcomer's hand.

"Looks that way. You all finished moving in?"

"I dropped some of my crap off earlier, but I won't actually be here until tomorrow. Feel free to set up anything you want. Put your stuff wherever. I'm not picky."

"Cool." Quinn unzipped his suitcase as Julian and I headed for the door. "See you around."

"Sure thing. See you tomorrow."

Julian and I made our way down the stairs and out into the parking lot. We climbed into his car and started our journey back home.

"Julian, when can we get Maggie registered? I need to get her insured and grab a parking pass."

"Maggie?" Much like Viktor, Julian didn't look at me as he drove.

"You know what I'm talking about. Maggie. I want to get her back on the road." Granted, the view from the passenger side of a Lexus was very nice, but it was nothing compared to the freedom of being in the driver's seat. Especially being in the driver's seat of a muscle car.

"Why would you want that old, beat-up relic?" He dared

a glance at me as he turned right out of campus. "I'm sure Viktor and I could help you find a newer car that's in better shape."

"There's more to it than that, Julian." It wasn't a matter of want, really. That car was the last real connection I had to my father. "Dad always said that if anything ever happened to him, I got Maggie. Viktor gave her to me, and all she needs now are new tires, a tune-up, and a good handwash. Besides, you can't say you really want to chauffeur me around all year, can you?"

Julian pulled his car into the garage and put it in park. "That car rolled off the assembly line seven years before I was born. It might not survive the school year."

"Let me worry about that." I grabbed Maggie's key from the box in the hall and headed out the door. I could barely hear Julian as I rounded the end of the house.

"Please be careful, Adrien. Don't get tetanus or anything." His voice continued to trail off as I made my way across the grounds toward the barn. Toward my Maggie. "Dinner is at six."

I pulled the hook from the latch and slid the barn door open. At one time, this barn had been used to house horses. But now it was storage for all sorts of items that Viktor didn't want to throw away, but wanted never to see. Boxes were piled atop pallets along either side, next to several pieces of furniture and old lamps that were covered by tarps. At the far end sat a large item, covered with a cloth tarp. Maggie. It had to be.

My feet moved soundlessly over the floor—slowly, even reverently, like I was in a place of worship. When I reached her, I placed my hand on the tarp that covered her and closed my eyes. A breath entered my lungs, deep and slow. With a longing that only a car guy could truly understand, I gripped a section of the tarp in my fist and pulled. The cloth moved over her back end, revealing that curvy black body I knew so well. Like a slinky dress unzipping and dropping to the floor, the tarp came free, revealing my sweet Maggie in all her glory.

"Well, don't you look pretty, you sweet thang, you." My lips lifted in a smile at the sight of her. She was the woman of my dreams, and we were together at last.

Despite the tarp, a thin layer of dust covered her, a few spots of it wiped away from where I'd removed the cloth. I wondered what she'd been up to in the past four years, my dirty girl, but the answer was obvious. Nothing. Nothing but waiting. Waiting for me.

As I stepped around to her driver's side door, I could see that Viktor had been right about her tires. But when I slid the key into the lock and opened up her door, I found nothing but perfection inside. Black leather, clean gauges. She looked ready to rock and roll. Pulling the hood lever, I got out and moved around to her front end. Her engine was just fine by the looks of it. She'd need a tune-up, of course. But she was in great shape, considering her long nap, and probably more than a little ready to get out of the barn. Girls like Maggie couldn't be satisfied by quiet nights at home. She needed to go out and tear hell through the world, leaving nothing but a dust cloud and gaping mouths in her wake.

Slipping off my hoodie, I dropped it on her roof and headed to the front of the barn. In the shelves to the right of the door were an assortment of paints, thinners, cleaning supplies, and everything I'd need for an oil change. I'd have to pick up the rest of the stuff for a tune-up next time I was in town. The tires were another issue. I was going to need new ones, and that meant asking Viktor for a loan. Tires weren't cheap, and I only had maybe ten bucks to my name. People always think that trust fund kids live high on the hog. So did I, until I became one. The way that my parents had set up my and Grace's trust, our schooling and everyday expenses were covered, but there would be no disbursement of any real money to us until we each hit the age of twenty-one. Until then, it was Broke City. Not that I was complaining. They'd given me a good life. I had nothing to complain about, really. Except for Grace.

After I opened the barn door for ventilation, I picked

up the oil pan and headed back to Maggie. I slid inside the driver's side door again, hoping like hell that she would start after such a long rest. When I slid the key into the ignition and turned it, her engine roared to life like it was nothing.

You couldn't stop a girl like Maggie from having a good time.

I let her run for a few minutes, listening happily to the roar of her engine, allowing her oil to warm. I cut her engine after a while and, once I'd gotten her up on jack stands, I put my earbuds in and cranked a bluesy playlist that I'd made before sliding underneath and unscrewing the drain plug. When the stream of oil had slowed to merely drops in the pan, I removed the oil filter and dumped the old oil out of it before putting it back on. I may not have been able to replace the filter just yet, but at least I could get rid of most of the used oil. I made a mental note to add that to my list for the auto parts store. I replaced the drain plug and dumped five bottles of 10W-30 into the engine. By the time I got Maggie off the jack, my hands were filthy and my heart was full. There was something deeply satisfying about car maintenance. I could see why my dad had loved it so much.

Pulling the tarp over Maggie again, I whispered promises to her that I would be back soon. And that next time, I'd polish her up real pretty and take her out on the town.

I kissed my filthy fingers and pressed them to her hood before turning to leave.

Humming a bit of the acoustic song "Going to Hell" by The Pretty Reckless, I made my way through a hot shower and dressed for dinner, my heart feeling lighter than it had in some time. I entered the dining room to find Viktor, Julian, and Grace waiting for me at the table. I again took my seat across from Grace, my stomach rumbling. Plates of rare pot roast and savory roasted carrots and potatoes were laid out before us on china plates. The smell of cherry crumble was wafting down the hall from the kitchen.

Julian smiled at me as I joined them. "How's Maggie?"

"Purring like a kitten. She'll be up and running in no time. Just you watch."

After a few bites, Viktor dabbed at his chin with his napkin. "So I hear your dorm room's in the tower, Adrien. What's it like up there? I'm afraid I haven't had a chance to see it since they finished the renovations."

I shrugged my shoulders. I was utterly unimpressed with the so-called renovations, but I didn't want to let Viktor in on my displeasure. It's not like complaining to him would change anything. "It's okay, I guess."

"Did you meet your roommate?" I couldn't exactly tell

if Viktor was getting at something or if he was just making polite dinner conversation.

"Yeah. His name's Quinn. He seems all right." Now for the test. I wasn't sure if Julian had had a chance to talk to her yet, so I was going out on a limb here and hoping for the best. "What about you, Grace? Did you meet your roommate?"

"I'm rooming with Penelope again." So far, so good. Her tone was even almost pleasant. "What classes are you in?"

"Honors Literature, AP Chemistry, AP Calculus, communication, economics, and biology."

I swirled a dinner roll around on my plate, sopping up the blood from the rare meat. So far, it was the longest civil dinner conversation in the history of our dinner conversations.

"You?"

"I'm taking regular chem and AP Bio. I'm in communication with you, though. Should prove interesting." That last bit had a hint of an edge to it. Not enough to really taste it, but enough that one might notice if it was left out of the recipe. I decided to tread lightly for the rest of the evening.

The conversation remained relatively tolerable throughout dinner. There were, of course, the occasional insults from Grace, but I let them pass. She thought she was being clever in the way that she tried to hide them within compliments, but she wasn't fooling anyone. And I was determined to keep my promise to Julian.

Dinner passed and dessert was served. I always loved the way that the vanilla bean ice cream pooled with the warm cherry crumble in the bottom of my bowl. The contrast between hot and cold, sweet and tart, made my taste buds happy. There would certainly not be anything this good in the cafeteria.

Finally, I stretched my arms over my head and yawned. "I think I'll turn in early. Thanks for the grub, Julian. It was delicious, as always. See you all in the morning."

With that, I made my way to the stairs. But I hadn't made it up the first two before footsteps from behind caught my attention. I thought maybe Julian was coming to thank me for letting so much go during dinner. But there was no way I could be so lucky.

"Adrien." Grace's voice was barely above a whisper. She looked over her shoulder to make sure that Viktor and Julian weren't listening. "I want to be clear that I'm only playing nice for Viktor. If he weren't dying, you and I wouldn't be speaking, and we certainly wouldn't be speaking cordially."

"Oh, I'm sorry. Was that what you call cordial?" I nodded toward the dining room. The look on her face told me that she knew exactly what I was talking about.

"More so than usual, you have to admit." The eye rolling

that accompanied her words said this was as good as I could expect to get. "Besides, we only have to pretend when we're around Viktor."

I couldn't believe her gall. "You say that like it was your idea, which is bullshit and we both know it. We're only acting civilly because Julian asked us to. Don't think I like it any more than you do."

Grace folded her arms across her chest and rolled her eyes again. Sometimes I wondered how they didn't roll right out of her head and across the floor.

"I'll tell you what, sis. You just stay out of my way and I'll stay out of yours. Deal?"

"Fine by me. Just make sure you hold up your end of that deal. Because if you get in my way at school, I don't intend to swerve. I'll plow right over you." With that, Grace stomped back into the dining room, and I climbed the stairs.

My phone buzzed in my pants pocket. When I pulled it out, there was a new text message, and I knew it was from the unknown number that had messaged me before because it appeared in the same chat window.

The papers she took are key. Find them.

I texted back. Who is this?

There was no reply.

[CHAPTER 4]

PARTIAL PRESSURE:
The pressure that would be exerted by one of the gases in a mixture if it occupied the same volume on its own

When I awoke the next morning, my mind was buzzing from a restless night of nightmares—some the usual back-to-school kind, and some not so much. I needed to get my ass back to California as soon as possible. It was bad enough when I'd thought being here would just mean having to see Grace around every turn. But it was getting harder to avoid thinking that she was part of some larger conspiracy. Even if it was coming from an anonymous source, the suggestion was enough to trigger some long-dormant anxieties about the deaths of my parents.

The texter had insinuated that Grace had had something to do with the lab accident that killed them. What if they were right? Proving her involvement would accomplish three things: 1. It would ease my mind, answering questions that had been haunting me for four years. 2. It would bring Grace to justice. Nothing would knock her off her high horse like a lifetime in prison. And 3. It would convince Viktor and Julian that I didn't belong at Wills anymore, so close to the scene of such a horrific crime.

One thing was certain. I was going about my issue with the mystery texter and the questions of what Grace might be up to behind my back in completely the wrong way. My mistake, which was now so apparent to me that it practically glowed in the dark, was not following scientific method to deal with the problem. In short, I needed to form a hypothesis—an educated guess that could be tested, accounting for the data at hand.

(I cringed whenever someone said they had a theory. They didn't have a theory—what they had was a hypothesis. It was enough to drive a thinking man mad.)

First I needed to collect my observations. Then I could evaluate those observations and imagine possible explanations, in order to judge which explanations were worthy of being hypotheses. With enough evidence to back up a hypothesis, I might be able to develop a solid theory as to what happened in my parents' lab that day, and what Grace was up to now.

I opened my top desk drawer and pulled out an old notebook and a pen. Flipping to the first page, I wrote the word *problem* at the top. Beneath it, I wrote *parents perished under unusual, as of yet unexplained conditions*. Beneath that, I wrote *observations*. My list of observations was short, but important. First, I noted the page that Grace had taken from our dad's journal, and her admission to stealing the other pages so that I wouldn't have them. Second, I listed the text messages, scrolling through my phone and writing them down word for word, marking each with a date and time, and noting where I was when I received them and what was going on around me.

At the top of the next page, I wrote *possible explanations*, and made another numbered list.

1. Grace was responsible, in large or in small part, for the demise of our parents.
2. Grace was not responsible for their deaths, but plans to benefit from them by taking our father's work for her own gain.

I took a deep breath as I wrote the next one, hoping like hell that it was wrong.

3. My anxiety has made me paranoid and I
am looking for anyone, anything, to blame
the unexplainable on.

After I was done, I shoved the notebook inside my duffel bag along with everything else I was taking with me to the dorms. It killed me to leave Maggie behind in the barn. I would have to get those new tires sooner than later.

For now, I had Julian drop me at the front door of the dorm, so at least I could walk in on my own. As expected, climbing the stairs to the tower was already getting old, and I could feel my legs aching. Some of my best friends in California were on the lacrosse team, but I'd never been much of an athlete myself. To be honest, I'd never really been much of anything. For years, teachers had lamented that if only I would apply myself, I could be capable of great things. But nothing had ever really sparked the drive in me that seemed to come so naturally to Grace. Honestly, I was just trying to get by. Survival mode. That's what I'd been in my entire life.

The door to my room creaked open with a push—apparently the renovations everyone was talking about didn't include squirting WD-40 on the hinges. The first thing I noticed was that Quinn had moved the furniture around since yesterday. My bed was tucked under the only window. My small desk sat beside it, the two divided only by one of the slanted, thick beams that came down from the low ceiling.

Quinn wasn't there, but he'd taken no time at all in getting settled in, and he'd taken my permission to do whatever he wanted to heart. His bed was wedged behind the door, covered in a quilt that looked like something out of *Doctor Who*. Tacked to the slanted beam on his side of the room were several photographs and bits of paper containing quotes that he'd either scribbled in a hurry or ripped from books. I read the first two I saw.

"I have learned more from my mistakes than from my successes."
                                                    —*Humphry Davy*

"Imagination is more important than knowledge."
                                                    —*Albert Einstein*

I went about putting the rest of my things away. Once my clothes were in the dresser, I made my bed and plugged in my laptop, opening it up and hitting the power button. I entered the Wi-Fi password I'd been handed with my class schedule and immediately went to the student directory on the school intranet. Some of the names looked familiar, but most didn't. It had been four years since I'd called the Wills Institute home, and most of the few friends I'd had back then were older and had since graduated. I was a stranger to the school now, just as it was a stranger to me. It seemed that a lot of Grace's friends from four years ago were still in attendance. I immediately felt outnumbered.

The door creaked open and I spun around to watch Quinn walk into the room, his arms full of books. As he dropped them on his bed, he smiled at me. "The bookstore is crazy right now. You might want to wait until after dinner to grab your supplies, if you don't have them already."

"Thanks for the tip, but I'm all set." I reached back and closed my laptop, guessing that now was as good a time as any to get to know the person I'd be living with, if only for a brief time. "So, Quinn . . . where ya from?"

"About five miles from here. You?" He began picking up his books and organizing them on top of his dresser. Something told me I wouldn't have to worry about having a messy roommate. In California, Connor had been a blast, but the guy had had no idea how to keep his laundry off the floor.

"Here. Kind of." He looked at me with a perplexed expression and I smiled. "I went to a boarding school out in San Diego for a few years, but I'm from here originally."

"What brought you back east? Senior year seems like a strange time to transfer." He opened a package of pens and slid them into a coffee mug next to the books before dropping the packaging in the small trash can beside his desk.

Inside my head, I saw Viktor—his cheeks sunken in,

his skin pale and sickly. He looked like I'd feared he would look when I first saw him upon my return. Attached to his arms were tubes. Covering the table beside him were bottles of pills. The image of my parents' lab flashed through my mind, too. I swore I could smell the burnt remains. Then there was Grace, sitting there all prim and proper. In her hands were the pages from my father's journal. The corner of her mouth lifted in a sadistic smirk. Shaking off the daydream with a shiver, I said, "Family stuff."

"Oh, don't get me started on family. You wouldn't believe my back story if I told you." He turned to face me, finished with tidying for the moment, and smiled. He was such a skinny little thing. Plaid shirt, wire-rimmed glasses. There was something familiar about his eyes, but I couldn't place it.

"I should tell you. I'll only be here a month. So you might get this room to yourself, unless they assign you a new roommate after I leave."

"A month? You're not staying through graduation?" He chewed his bottom lip for a moment, a distracted glint in his eyes.

"I really have to get back. Wills . . . it's just not where I want to be."

He nodded slowly and then said, "Hey, you wanna hit the dining hall? Grab some lunch? Hang out for a bit?"

"Sure." We headed out the door and I locked it behind us. The hallway was bustling with students enjoying their last day before classes as we made our way down the stairs to the main floor of the tower. "So how long have you been at Wills?"

"This is my first year here, actually. But I'm a senior."

We navigated through the flow of freshmen and boxes until we hit the front door that would lead us outside. "Any particular reason you transferred in for senior year?"

He shrugged. "The truth is, Wills is pretty prestigious. And a school with a rep like this one has looks a hell of a lot better on college applications than the school I was going to. Until this semester, I was in public school and spending my weekends volunteering at the hospital where my mom works. I'm trying to change my life."

We made our way across the lawn, toward the student center and the dining hall. I opened the door and held it for him. "Well, we can be aliens together for a while."

"Aliens?"

Faces passed—many familiar—but no one made eye contact with me. Finally, a guy name Gregg passed by. I opened my mouth to say hi—we'd been friendly enough in middle school—but he cut me off by purposefully slamming his shoulder into mine. My jaw tightened in irritation, but I didn't say anything. Honestly, I didn't know what to say. The last I knew, Gregg and I had been completely cool.

I looked at Quinn again. "I'm feeling a bit like I landed on another planet here."

Quinn slapped me on the shoulder. And even though we'd only just met, and he had no real knowledge of my past, I got the feeling that he understood. "I hear ya, Captain."

I looked at him with uncertain eyes. "Captain?"

The expression on Quinn's face was matter-of-fact. As though there should have been no question what he was talking about. "Yeah. You know. Star Trek. Which captain do you prefer, Kirk or Picard?"

Shaking my head as I entered the dining hall, I said, "A conversation for another time. Come on, redshirt. Let's grab something to eat."

The dining hall was the most standout building on campus. Back when Wills was built, it was a religious school, and what was now the dining hall was then the chapel. About fifty years ago, the school went completely nonsectarian. But the chapel was such an architectural asset that the school decided to keep it and convert it to the kitchen and dining hall. Large arched wooden doors greeted diners. The walls inside were stone, matching the outside, but decorated with large paintings of the various headmasters who had served the Wills Institute since the school's inception. Along the back wall was a line of heated and chilled food servers, and ten rows of long plank tables filled the room. Overhead, three gigantic wrought-iron chandeliers hung, giving the entire space a Gothic feel.

Quinn and I moved to the buffet on the back wall and grabbed trays, filling our plates with helpings of fried chicken, potatoes, green beans, and globs of yellow stuff that looked all right. After we picked up some silverware and napkins, we took seats at a mostly empty table.

That's when I noticed Grace, tall and confident and at the center of her group of friends. They passed by our table as if we didn't exist.

I tried to ignore her, but Quinn found that notion impossible. He was staring. "Wow. She looks like the queen bee."

"Insect or alphabetical letter?"

"I meant like . . . like a bee. So . . . insect, I guess." He looked lost for a moment, but then seemed to make the connection that she and I knew each other. "Why? You privy to some inside info that I'm not?"

"She's definitely an insect. I'll give you that much." I shoveled a bite of the yellow stuff into my mouth. It turned out to be banana pudding.

"Too bad. She's really hot." His eyes followed her until she disappeared behind the buffet table. "Insect or not, she's got a great thorax."

"She's my sister."

Quinn was looking at me again. Surprise, shame, and fear filled his eyes. "Dude, I'm sorry. I didn't know."

"Don't worry about it. We're not exactly close." I took the final bite of banana pudding and reminded myself to take a larger portion next time.

Quinn's eyes found Grace again as she and her friends took their seats at another table. "I should have known. You two have a similar cheekbone structure."

That made me laugh. "Now, I'd like to know how that happened."

This time Quinn's expression was confused. "Genetics, Captain."

"I was adopted."

Quinn blushed slightly. This conversation just wasn't going his way. "Oh. Sorry."

I shook my head. It didn't matter. It wasn't the first time someone had said that Grace and I looked similar, and I was certain that it wouldn't be the last. "Her name is Grace."

"Does she have any?"

"Grace?" I didn't bother to look at my sister, though it seemed that Quinn was having a hard time looking anywhere else. "Physically, yes. She's very prim, very proper. As far as inside? Not much that I've seen. That is, of course, unless you're one of her loyal subjects."

"Wow." He bit off the end of a roll and chewed, looking

thoughtfully between my sister and me. Grace was chatting with her friends. I was glad that she had decided to sit as far away from me as possible, but I was also trying not to think about it. She could sit wherever she wanted to sit. I didn't care.

Quinn looked like he was watching a tennis match. His eyes moved back and forth between us, scrutinizing. It was clear that his mind was working overtime trying to figure us out, to no avail. Finally, his eyes settled on me, as if he were studying the results of an experiment.

It wasn't easy to keep the annoyance from my tone. "What?"

"I've just never heard anyone speak with such bitterness about their sister before."

My plate of food had remained relatively untouched since I'd finished my pudding. The subject of my sister had this funny way of stealing my appetite. "What do you mean? A lot of people don't get along with their sisters."

Quinn pointed at me with his spoon. Apparently he had just sampled the banana pudding as well. "It's not what you say, it's how you say it. She must've really done a number on you at some point."

"Let's just say that it's complicated. Bottom line is that I don't trust her." This topic of conversation was sending pinpricks up the back of my neck, so I opted to change it.

"What about you? Have any siblings?"

Now it was Quinn's turn to look uncomfortable. "A half brother and half sister. But we don't really get along. I mean, my sister doesn't speak to me. And my brother . . . well, we're not really close."

I cracked open a can of Mountain Dew. I might not have been hungry anymore, but there was nothing that could ruin my love for the citrus splash of cold Dew. "I wonder if part of the problem is the whole boarding-school thing."

"What do you mean?" He licked the yellow goop from his spoon and made a face. Apparently, he was not as much a fan of the banana pudding as I was.

"Well, you and your siblings, me and Grace. There's a definite lack of closeness in a family when you all go to boarding schools." I leaned back in my chair, propping my foot on the empty chair across the table from me. "Think there might be a connection?"

"Maybe." He shrugged. "But in my case, I think parental bullshit has definitely gotten in the way."

"Favoritism?"

"Definitely."

Grace was seated several tables away, laughing at something that one of her friends had said. Her laughter was soft and pleasant, but my ears translated it as shrill. It was funny how like and dislike of people could change the way that they sounded in your head. "I never had that on my end. My mom and dad always treated Grace and me as equals, despite the adoption. Neither of us was the favorite, as far as I could tell. Grace just never liked me. Not even when we were toddlers."

"That sucks, dude." He spoke over a mouthful of mashed potatoes. Something told me Quinn didn't get a lot of action. If any. "Let's talk about something else. What do you plan on doing when you graduate?"

Actually, I hated this question. It wasn't that I didn't know what I wanted to do with my life. It was just boring. The kind of question people asked when they ran out of things to say. Like *How's the weather?* or *Nice day, isn't it?* I tipped up the green can, draining its contents. "I'd like to get a degree in chemistry. My dad was a chemist. I'd love to follow in his footsteps. If not that . . . I dunno. Maybe I'll become a car mechanic or something. To be honest, I don't really know what I'm gonna do after high school. What about you?"

He shrugged as he swallowed his potatoes. Then he picked up his soda can and said, "I'm torn. Part of me enjoys the idea of becoming a forensic pathologist. You know, cutting up dead people and figuring out how they died? But the other part of me just wants to chuck it all and live in a van."

I couldn't contain the horrified expression I had to be

wearing when he said it. "Like a minivan? Like a mom-mobile?"

It was all he could do not to spit soda out of his nose. "Hell no! Like one of those giant monstrosities from the seventies with the ridiculously huge murals painted on the side. Like Zeus throwing lightning at a village of psyche-delic angels or Satan having a barbecue with a group of pigs. You know. Something messed up like that."

"Sounds like a good time." It didn't. Not really. But you know—to each their own and all that.

"Yeah. Something to do until I come to my senses and get a job and a place and a life. Y'know?"

There, I knew exactly what he was talking about. Some people, the lucky few, had a solid plan for how their life was meant to pan out. But the rest of us—most of us—had no clue what tomorrow might bring.

Across the room, Grace and her friends were suddenly having quite the animated chat. Several of them were look-ing over at me, but I had no idea what they might be talking about. Still, I tried not to care. Why should I? They were her friends, not mine. If I gave a crap what anybody thought of me, it was in this order: 1. Myself, and 2. Anybody I deemed worthy enough to include in my life. I pulled my attention away from Grace and her crew, back to Quinn.

He'd given up on the cafeteria food and pushed his tray

away from him. "You ever daydream about the stupid shit you'd do if you didn't have to make a responsible choice for your future?"

"No. Can't say I have." And it was true. I didn't know what exactly I wanted to do, but that didn't mean I wasn't trying to figure it out. In the back of my mind, my dad's voice echoed, *"You need direction in your life, Adrien. You're such a bright young man. If only you'd just apply yourself."*

"Well then." Quinn smiled at me as he reached for the macadamia nut cookie on my tray. "It looks like I've got a month to fix that."

I didn't have the heart to tell him, but if my idea of a good life was something a guy like Quinn could fix for me, I was in big trouble.

Locks of bright red hair caught my eye as a familiar curvaceous figure passed behind Quinn. I looked up and put on my best smile. "Hey, Sherry. Long time no see."

I guess you could say that Sherry had been my first girlfriend. We made out in the hallway during the seventh-grade formal dance. Hers were the first boobs I'd ever touched. To be honest, they'd also been the last.

Sherry turned toward the sound of my voice, looking as though she was bothered by the intrusion. I blinked, hoping she'd recognize me. "Adrien Dane?" I said. "Remember me? We went to the seventh-grade Snow Ball together."

"Yeah, sorry." The look on her face suggested that there might have been a foul odor in the air, but I was pretty sure it was just me that had that effect on her. She turned away and walked off.

I couldn't be sure if she was apologizing for not remembering me, or saying she was sorry she'd gone to the dance with me. My second life at the Wills Institute wasn't off to a good start. I wondered what Grace had been saying about me in the past four years. If she'd been poisoning ears, I had major damage control to attend to. Otherwise, my time here was going to be miserable and stretch on into eternity—which is what freshman year was supposed to be like. Not senior.

Quinn said, "Nice girl."

"She used to be." Sherry sashayed away in the direction of the front door.

"So what was California like?" One thing was for sure. Quinn was a chatty companion. I had a feeling I was going to have to invest in several cases of Tylenol if we were going to spend much time together. But then, some people can't just sit in the quiet and be. Some people can't resist the urge to fill the quiet with noise. I liked the quiet. It gave me time to think. Or not think. Depending on my mood.

"Warm. Good school. Nice people. I liked it. I mean, who doesn't like palm trees, am I right?"

"Must've been hard to leave."

"Yeah. But it was important I come back. My guardian is pretty sick. He asked me to. So I did."

"Guardian?" The word was almost indistinguishable coming from around the cookie in his mouth.

"Legal guardian. My godfather. My parents passed away a few years ago. One of the reasons I moved to California."

"I'm so sorry."

The mashed potatoes on my tray were starting to take the shape of a rather impressive volcano. All I needed now were some peas to represent the citizens of Pompeii. "It happens."

It seemed to be the mention of dead parents that finally slowed Quinn's appetite. "Listen, do you wanna maybe check out the Hub or something? I've heard that's kind of the place to be around here."

Apparently, we weren't the only ones who had finished eating. Grace had broken away from her clan and was heading for the exit. She made sure to cast me a venomous glance as she passed. "Actually, if you don't mind, I'll catch up with you later."

There was something about the way that Grace was carrying herself that piqued my interest. I could see that her friends were as confused as I was about why she was leaving them. And there was something different about her as she left the dining hall. Something suspicious. Something sneaky. Normally I would have just dismissed it. But with everything else that had been going on, I felt like I needed to find out what she was up to.

I followed Grace across the school grounds. She passed right by the dorms, so I knew that she wasn't on her way back to her room. I was careful to stay out of sight, ducking behind trees and hiding in the shadows. The last thing I wanted was for Grace to catch me spying on her. She made her way into the library and headed straight out the back door. I was about to follow her when a hand grabbed my shoulder, spinning me around.

"Adrien Dane. I can't believe you're here." It was Penelope, Grace's roommate. I hadn't seen her since before I left Wills four years ago. She didn't like me much then, either. "When Grace told me you were coming back, I was in absolute shock. You've got some nerve, you know that?"

"It's nice to see you, too, Penelope." I could only hope that she hadn't seen me following Grace. If she had seen that, I was screwed for sure. "What do you mean, nerve?"

"Coming back here after what you did." She poked me in the chest with a perfectly manicured nail a little harder than I thought she was capable of.

"What exactly did I do?"

"You totally abandoned your sister after what happened

to your parents. She was left all alone, without any family at all." A second poke in the same spot.

I rubbed my sternum at the site of Penelope's digital assault. "Is that the story she's been spreading around? Because that's not exactly how it happened."

"You're just a heartless jerk, if you ask me." Her hand was poised for another poke. Luckily, mine was still rubbing my chest, blocking her attack.

"Well, I don't recall asking you." I had more important things to do than to sit here and be berated by my sister's "bestie." Finding out exactly what my sister was up to, for starters. "Now, if you'll excuse me."

I made my way out the back door to the library, but Grace was already long gone. I wasn't surprised. She had seemed like a woman on a mission. I guessed I'd have to wait for another opportunity to find out what that mission entailed.

I crossed to the parking garage behind the library and made my way to the back of campus. The school sat on several acres, some of which were heavily wooded. There was even a small lake on the property. I remember when we were first accepted to Wills, how my dad had gone on and on about the ecosystems that we would be able to explore in our biology classes and how excited Mom got when she thought about the indigenous plant life in the forest. More important for me, it made for a great place to walk when you wanted to clear your head. Not many students came out this way unless they were with a class. That is, of course, unless they were getting private lessons in anatomy from one another. But those students tended to stick to the dense parts of the woods where it was easier to hide from the security guards. Walking by the lake was a relatively safe bet.

I walked for probably an hour or more, stopping every now and then to skip a stone or watch a bat fly over the glasslike water, darting this way and that in search of a meal. So many thoughts ran through my mind. What was Grace up to? Why did she take those pages from Dad's journal? Where were those pages now? Who was sending me the text messages? How did that mystery person know so much? Why wouldn't they just come out and tell me what was going on?

There was one question that stuck out in my mind more than any other. I hadn't thought about it in years. But being back here at the Wills Institute, back at the place where I had first heard the news, brought it to the forefront of my mind. And now I needed to know the answer more than ever. I needed to know what had happened that day at my parents' lab. The official report listed it as an accident, likely attributed to the mislabeling of some pretty volatile chemicals. There was no more detail than that in the report. But it had to be wrong. My parents were too careful to let something like that happen. My father's obsessive nature extended much further than his journal. He was just as meticulous, if not more, in his lab work. There was something more to their deaths than what was being told, and I needed to find out what.

I had thought that taking a walk would clear my head, but it seemed to have had the opposite effect. Now I needed to lie down. I made my way back to the main part of campus and into the lobby of the tower. A few kids were lounging in the common room playing video games. A student teacher sat at the front desk listening to the campus radio station. Today must have been the first day it was back on the air for the year. I recognized the unmistakable guitar playing of Billie Joe Armstrong as the Green Day song faded, only to be replaced by an equally familiar voice. A voice that I hadn't heard in four years, and one that I was very happy to hear.

I darted out of the tower and made my way back to the library. Skipping the wait for the elevator, I ran up the three flights of stairs to where the radio station was located. Sitting behind the window was Josh Davies, my roommate and best friend from the last time I was at Wills. Other than his dark hair being a bit longer and his left ear being pierced, he looked exactly the same. It was great to see him doing his thing on the radio. He looked right at home. It had always been his dream. I couldn't count how many times I'd walked in on him practicing into a hairbrush between songs on his iPod.

I waited for the red *ON AIR* light to go off before I opened the studio door. I couldn't stop my lips from curling into a smile at the sight of my best friend. A worry crossed my mind that he might not like me anymore, but I pushed it away.

"Some things never change."

Josh pulled the headphones off his ears as he turned. His green eyes were as bright and sharp as I remembered them. "No way. Adrien friggin' Dane. How the hell have you been, man?"

I was greeted with a warm hug. It seemed that Josh was the only person I had known before I left who was happy to see me. Other than Viktor and Julian, of course.

"Good, good. How are you?" I patted him on the back as we parted from our embrace. For some reason, that's what men did. They could hug, but they had to pat each other on the back when they did so. It was kind of the this-is-not-a-romantic-thing signal. I was pretty sure that Viktor and Julian didn't pat each other on the back when they hugged.

I couldn't stop smiling.

He said, "Let's see, the last time I saw you, you'd singed your eyebrows off trying to create water with a balloon filled with helium, a balloon filled with oxygen, and an open flame." Josh rubbed his eyebrows for emphasis. He was smiling, too.

"I'm still pretty sure it worked. But the fireball kinda evaporated it."

"They grew back in okay. So what are you doing here? I thought you'd be spending your entire senior year lounging on a beach."

A chuckle escaped me. "What? Give up snow and gray skies for a year-round tan and palm trees? It's like you don't know me at all."

"Smartass. You haven't changed a bit." He held up a finger and put his headphones back on. I took a seat in the chair next to him. Flipping a switch, Josh spoke into the microphone. "That was Panic! at the Disco on WILS radio. This is Josh Davies. Just give me a call or shoot me a text message if there's anything you want to hear. You know the number, people. This next one was requested by Stacie over there in Vandercook Hall."

He flipped another switch and took off his headphones. He started talking again like there hadn't been a break in our conversation. "If you must know, I'm still kinda pissed at you for bailing on me."

My chest ached some with the weight of the guilt. "Look, I'm sorry about ditchin' out. I just—"

"Dude. I'm totally screwing with ya." Josh grinned and smacked me playfully on the knee. "It's good to have you home again."

"Did I miss anything exciting?"

"Just the usual—I'm currently skating through high school on a C average and keeping the parental fury at bay while I prepare for what I really wanna do."

I raised an eyebrow at him. The last thing I knew, Josh had wanted to be a rock star. A shame he couldn't play guitar or sing. "Which is?"

"You're looking at it, dude. I wanna be a DJ. Like a radio DJ. Professionally."

Watching the man work, I could tell that he was serious. "That's . . . cool."

"You say it like I've decided to willingly contract some horrible disease or something." Josh was moving all around the studio checking the text messages on the computer, looking up songs, readying commercials for the next set. There was no denying it—he was good at what he did.

"That's not it. I'm just . . . I dunno . . . surprised."

"I love doing it. Sure, it won't make me a lot of money. But there are more important things than cash, y'know?"

All I could do was sit back and watch in amazement. "I guess I'm just wondering why you still bother with a school like Wills if that's what you wanna do. It's so much tougher here."

Josh rolled his eyes as he pulled an LP out of its dust jacket. "My dad wants me to be a district attorney. My mom wants me to go into medicine. I'm seventeen. Which means that my life doesn't even belong to me for another six months. So if my parents say I go to Wills, and they daydream about me being a doctor or some other ridiculously out-there crap despite my grades, then I just ride the ride until I board the freedom train."

The presence of an actual vinyl album took me aback for a second. "Dude, do you still use those? I thought everything was digital now."

Josh gingerly placed the LP onto the turntable and placed the needle onto one of the grooves. "Most everything is, but every now and then we DJs get nostalgic."

"What the hell do you mean, *nostalgic*?" I couldn't help but roll my eyes a little bit. "You're seventeen, dude. You were born in the era of CDs and MP3s."

He nodded. "Yeah, but these have a really great sound to them. And when one of the teachers requests a song from Journey, you gotta give them what they want. Don't stop believin', Adrien."

With the flip of another switch, the turntable started spinning. "What about you? Still planning to be a chemist?"

I was pretty impressed he remembered. "I have no idea what I'm doing. Other than getting out of here as soon as possible."

"What are you doing here, man?" Josh had known me better than anyone else at Wills. He knew why I'd left. "Why the hell did you come back? You were out. You were free."

"Not my choice, really. I was kind of backed into a corner that I couldn't avoid. So. I'm here." I could have brought up Viktor, but for one brief moment, I just wanted to forget about the bad in my life. And Josh had always been great for that. I leaned back in my chair and sighed. "For a place that looks so much like it did four years ago, things sure seem to have changed, eh?"

"Yeah." His voice was suddenly serious. "I can't imagine people are being very nice to you, huh?"

I thought about Gregg slamming his shoulder into mine and Sherry obviously brushing me off—not to mention Penelope's lecture. "Not exactly."

"It's because of Grace." He flipped another switch, but didn't bother to pick up the headphones. In the background I could hear advertisements for the bookstore and an announcement about the first school dance of the year. "After . . . what happened . . . with your parents, I mean . . . the whole school was in mourning for you guys. And then Grace came back, and you didn't. And everyone saw Grace dealing with the loss of your parents on her own. To them, it looked like you just stepped out on your only family. To some, it looked like maybe you had something to do with it. And your sister didn't do anything to stop those rumors. If anything, she fueled them."

I closed my eyes in frustration. "Fantastic. So everyone hates me."

"Not everyone." He gave me a wink. "I mean, I still think you're okay."

"You hittin' on me?" A daring smile crossed my lips.

"Maybe. I am pretty desperate. Who got stuck with you as a roommate, anyway?"

"Some new guy named Quinn. Seems okay. A little excited, maybe. But the noobs always are."

Josh held out a hand and helped me stand up. "You comin' to First Night?"

I let out a small groan. "From what you just told me, I'm the school pariah. Why on earth would I subject myself to that?"

"Because it's tradition. Besides, if you don't go, then people will just despise you more." His attention was back on his work. The commercial messages were almost over and more requests had come through on his phone.

"I'm not sure I care." I thought that if I kept telling myself that, sooner or later I might start to believe it.

"Yeah, you do. And PS, you're a shitty liar." He typed a song title into the computer and added it to the queue.

I sighed. If I couldn't even fool myself, how was I supposed to fool anyone else? "Same time? Same place?"

"Tomorrow at midnight on the riverbank clearing just off campus. Bring something. Or someone."

"I don't have anyone." I'd been out of town for four years and back in town for three days. Where, exactly, was I supposed to meet anyone in that time frame?

"I can introduce you to some people."

It was clear that Josh and I were going to have to get to know each other all over again. "What if I don't want to meet any girls?"

He shrugged. "I never said girls. I can introduce you to some boys, too. Hey man, I don't judge."

"I appreciate that." I stood and made my way toward the door. It was getting late, and I was getting tired. "I still don't know if I'm going."

"Like I said, you're a shitty liar. See you tomorrow night." Josh flipped the switch and spoke into the microphone again. He was back in his element. I slowly and quietly opened the door, then made my way down the stairs and out the library door. If what Josh said was true, this month back at Wills was going to be a lot harder than I had thought.

CHAPTER 5

SURFACE TENSION:

The elastic tendency of liquids,
which makes them acquire the
least surface area possible

The science lab at Wills was probably the most recently renovated of all the classrooms. The eight tables were made of shiny, flawless steel, with a sink at each station and two drawers on either side, stuffed with various supplies like gloves and masks. At the front of the classroom was a smart board that must have cost a pretty penny. To the right of the door was an eyewash station. Lining the back wall were several tall lockable cabinets containing various chemicals in jars. At the end of the row of cabinets was the door to the supply closet, where the more caustic chemicals were stored.

I'd always loved labs. Just standing in one transported

me back several years to my father's side. He would wear his crisp white lab coat and direct me to stir different chemicals together. I could almost see him now, could almost feel his hand patting me gently on the back as he said, *"Adrien, you have to make your measurements exact, and be careful to watch what chemicals you mix. Chemistry is magical, but also dangerous."*

I shook my head, bringing myself back to the present. I tried not to think of my parents too often. The pain was too much to bear.

Mr. Meadows stood at the front of the classroom. He looked very young to be a teacher at Wills. In fact, if it weren't for the fact that he wore a full beard, he probably would have been able to blend in with the students in the halls. As we filed in and took our seats, he watched us suspiciously, as if sorting us into categories of "good student" and "poor student" before he'd even gotten to know us as individuals. I walked in second to last, and as I made my way past the few remaining open seats, I was greeted with bitter glances. One girl went so far as to set her purse in the chair next to her to prevent me from joining her. Finally, I reached the back of the room and sat beside a quiet, withdrawn girl who seemed more interested in whatever thoughts were occupying her mind at the time than who might sit beside her.

"Ladies and gentlemen, my pack rat of a stepfather

recently passed from here to the great beyond. To listen to him tell it, he was the owner and purveyor of a rather successful reclamation company. But whatever description you choose to believe, I am now the unfortunate recipient of all of his rusted, dusty belongings. Among those, I have in my possession six cast-iron bathtubs. I have no need of one cast-iron bathtub, let alone six. Therefore, our first project will be to destroy them however you see fit, using chemistry as your guide."

Mr. Meadows stood at the front of our class. He wasn't dressed the way that most Wills teachers dressed. No suits or ties for him. His hair was long and wild—I seemed to recall him wearing it in a braid or a ponytail, but not today. He wore jeans and motorcycle boots, and to top off his ensemble, he wore a Grateful Dead shirt that looked as if he'd purchased it back when the Grateful Dead had first hit the music scene. If any other teacher had dressed the way Mr. Meadows did, or taught the way Mr. Meadows did, they would have been fired in a heartbeat.

But Mr. Meadows had a reputation for being extremely generous to the school with his vast inheritance, and also for being completely mad. "In short, you will pair up, compute which chemical or chemicals to use and in what measurements, perform small tests to prove your theories to yourselves, and then, with the blessing of our very open-minded headmaster . . . we are going to blow shit up."

He paused as we all exchanged uncertain glances, and then threw up an impatient arm. "Well? Acquaint yourselves."

The willowy girl next to me was thin, with straight, long blond hair so light that it almost matched her pale skin. Her eyes were light blue, and something about her reminded me of a watercolor painting. There were no hard lines, no definite edges. She was who she was, a softly blended vision of a teenage girl.

I turned toward her and smiled. "Hey. I'm Adrien."

"Looks like you got stuck with the leftovers." She didn't look sad or mad or anything that might indicate that she wasn't happy about me being her partner. It was just a strange statement of what she believed to be factual.

"Funny, I thought you were the one who got stuck with me." It was clear that we both knew exactly where we stood on the social ladder of the student body. "So, do you have a lot of experience with alkali metals?"

"Some. But if you're looking for coattails to ride, you got stuck with the wrong girl. I only barely skated into this class and don't have high hopes for my survival, if you want to know the truth." She met my eyes, her tone even and calm. It was as if she had no volume button, no passion. She was logical, literal, and apparently lived in a world defined by her observations. "I'm just saying, don't look for me to carry you, because if that's what you're counting on, you're screwed. Royally, as it were."

Even though I got the impression that I should be insulted, I was more intrigued than anything. Not to mention more than a little relieved that she seemed to have no idea who I was, or didn't care. "Don't worry, I think I have a pretty steady grasp on the subject."

"Yeah. That's what they all think. And then, blammo."

"I'm pretty sure I'll do okay." Okay. I didn't want to brag, but chemistry was the one class I did better than okay in. I'd started assisting my dad in the lab when I was only eight, and for fun at home, my family had discussed the chemical compositions of various items around the house. To say I'd do okay was a gross understatement. But I didn't want to brag, considering I'd just met her. "Chemistry is pretty easy to understand once you grasp the basics. I may be crap at every other class, but I've got this."

To my amazement, she laughed. Loudly. Attracting the attention of everyone in the room, including Mr. Meadows. "Something amusing going on at table five?"

Her laughter ceased as quickly as it had started. "I think my partner is a robot. Or deluded into thinking he's Alfred Nobel or something."

Mr. Meadows crossed his arms in front of him, eyeing me with a faint sense of recognition. "You look familiar, boy, but I suspect you're not Alfred Nobel. What's your name?"

"Adrien." I hesitated before saying my last name. I wasn't sure why. "Dane."

"Oh." In a single moment, it all came flooding back to him. He knew very well who I was, who my parents were, and what had happened. "I was sorry to hear of your father's passing. He was a brilliant chemist and an accomplished instructor here at Wills. And your mother was the most talented botanist I have ever had the fortune of knowing. You're quite lucky to have Adrien as a partner, Ms. . . ."

"Caroline Stanton." Her voice was quiet—just a touch above a whisper—and she seemed angry about something, but I couldn't be certain what. Maybe she was just embarrassed.

"Ms. Stanton. If Adrien is even half as bright as his parents, you should have no trouble getting a respectable grade on this project."

Now it was my turn to be angry. "Excuse me. Her name is Caroline. If you're going to address me by my first name, it seems only polite you call her by hers. And she'll get the grade because she'll earn it. Now, I believe you owe her an apology."

Mr. Meadows stared at me in shock. His cheeks turned

a shade of pink as the truth of what I'd said flooded through him.

"I apologize, Ms. . . ." He caught himself and said, "Caroline."

As Mr. Meadows returned to the front of the class, she said, "Thanks."

"No problem."

She met my eyes, and I could see the blue in hers had deepened in anger. "Now I'm marked for the rest of the semester. As if this class wasn't going to be hard enough without the teacher hating me."

"Hey." I couldn't believe she was chastising me for helping her. What was wrong with this girl? "I meant what I said. You were smart enough to get into this class, right? You're gonna do just fine. And what you can't figure out . . . well . . . maybe I can."

"I don't need help from a guy like you, and I certainly don't need your pity." She sat back in her chair, folding her arms in front of her. "And I don't put out, either."

My jaw hit the ground. What the hell was she talking about? I pulled out a notebook and flipped it open, picking up a pen so I could get to work on some notes for this ridiculous project—with or without her help. Under my breath, I muttered, "Screw me for trying to be nice."

"I said I don't put out." I looked at her, ready to explain

it was a figure of speech, but was met with a small smile. "Thanks. For real this time. I can stick up for myself, but I appreciate the sentiment."

I blushed and shrugged. I could tell this girl was going to keep me on my toes. We pulled out books and both started looking up things and making a few notes. It seemed like the other lab pairs didn't really know where to begin, but I had a few ideas. "So," I said. "Alkali metals. How do you feel about sodium, Caroline?"

"It's okay. But nothing gets me hotter than magnesium." She raised an eyebrow at me. "Get it? Oh come on, that's funny."

It *was* funny. She was funny. In a strange, where-the-hell-did-this-girl-come-from sort of way. Her moods seemed to shift like the clouds on a windy day. Unpredictable. Unstable. There was something about that that appealed to me. Most people were naturally attracted to sweet or sour, to light or dark, to self-preservation or throwing caution to the wind. I liked the fact that she might be both, or all, or none at once.

Shaking my head, I said, "Seriously, though. Sodium—"

"Magnesium burns at 3,600 degrees Fahrenheit and at close distance is brighter than the sun. I mean, that crap can burn a hole through a car's engine block. It can certainly take care of some old guy's bathtub." She looked at me with a challenge in her eyes. One that sent a rather pleasant chill through my bones. To be honest, I enjoyed a good argument.

"Magnesium is hot, yes, but if my understanding of the project is correct, our goal isn't to melt the tub. It's to decimate it."

Inside my mind, I could see my father mixing one liquid with another in his lab. The combined chemicals began to smoke, and the smoke was sucked up into the chemical hood. He shook his head, disappointed, and said to me, *"What did I say? Dangerous."*

"What about thermite? It certainly did a number on the *Hindenburg*."

That it did. Once it caught fire, the *Hindenburg* dirigible burned from back to front in under thirty-eight seconds. Thermite was certainly nothing to mess with—unless you knew what you were doing. Even so, I shook my head. "You're still thinking hot, not reactive. We need something that will explode. Which is why I suggested sod—"

"What about potassium?" A light switch flipped on inside my mind when she said the word, illuminating all sorts of wonderful ideas. The results would be spectacular. "I mean . . . like sodium, it's so reactive with water that it has to be stored in oil because it will react with the moisture in the air. But it has a bit more . . . I dunno . . . punch, I think.

We could give old Mr. Meadows quite a show with enough potassium. Don't you think?"

I smiled. "Potassium it is."

"Plus, potassium is way prettier to watch react. All those blues and purples." She looked kind of daydreamy when she spoke of the chemical. If I was drawn to her before, I really liked her now.

"So . . . listen. Are you busy tonight?"

"I'm not going to First Night, if that's what you're asking."

Furrowing my brow, I asked, "Why not?"

"Because it's a stupid tradition and I have better things to do. Don't you?"

The bell rang and, without another word or even waiting for my response, Caroline picked up her books and headed out the door with the rest of the class. I took a deep breath and released it, speaking into the air what I'd been about to say to her. "Apparently not."

I headed back to my dorm room around three thirty. Quinn looked up from his desk as I walked in the door. He said, "How was day one?"

I wanted to say something about how it had been blissfully Grace-free, but instead just shrugged. That was none of his business. And as for how my classes had been . . . it was only the first day. Which meant that they weren't anything yet.

I didn't mention Caroline, but I was thinking about her. Even though I was trying not to.

Quinn groaned. "I just slogged through an hour of calculus. Ugh. It may kill me. It may literally kill me by the end of the semester."

"I doubt anyone has actually died because of a complex mathematics system." I set my books on my desk and nodded thoughtfully. "But if they have, it was probably calculus that killed them."

"It's like learning to speak a different language from another planet or something. I'm great at math. Why is this so damn intimidating? Arrrgh." He laid his head on his calculus book and groaned some more.

"You'll live."

"Yeah, but my GPA may not make it out alive. And it's teetering on the brink of the college-acceptance threshold as it is."

"It's the first day. Cut yourself some slack." In a moment that I was certain I'd come to regret, I said, "Hey, Quinn? You busy tonight?"

"No, why?"

"Well, it's just that there's a tradition at Wills called First Night. The staff knows about it, but turn their heads as long as we keep it off campus. It's a big party with a bonfire on the riverbank. There's music and everybody just kinda cuts loose before school really gets heavy. I thought maybe you'd wanna check it out. It's a good way to make friends, meet people. Y'know."

He sat up, looking a little more than eager. Something told me he didn't get out much. I could only hope he wouldn't talk my ear off all night. "Yeah, man. That sounds great."

It occurred to me that I wasn't inviting Quinn out of kindness or friendship. The air at Wills had changed since I'd last been here. I'd never exactly been Mr. Popularity, but I had used to be greeted by smiles at least. Now I was either invisible or a thorn in several sides. There was no way I wanted to show up to First Night on my own. So yeah, maybe I was using Quinn. But I had my reasons.

"Cool. It starts at midnight. We can walk over together."

[CHAPTER 6]

IONIC BOND:

A chemical bond between two
ions with opposite charges

It had been four years since I'd made this walk across the moonlit campus through the thickly grown woods to the river, but it felt like it might as well have been four days. The walk was so familiar, so unchanged, and it occurred to me as Quinn and I moved through the trees that the midnight walk to First Night was as much a part of the tradition as the celebration itself. The walk was leaving things behind. The party was about moving forward. I'd heard First Night had been taking place at the same time, at the same place, for over fifty years. My parents had met at First Night. Josh and I had tasted our first beer at First Night our sixth-grade year. To outsiders, First Night might just seem like some lame party thrown by a bunch of spoiled private school kids. But to me, to all the kids at Wills, First Night was about beginnings. And if I needed anything this year, it was a new beginning.

The music reached us before we'd even made it out of the woods. But we couldn't see the glow from the towering bonfire on the water's edge until we broke through the tree line. All along the riverbank the students of Wills Institute were gathered. Some sat on blankets they'd laid out on the ground, some sat atop coolers or in lawn chairs they'd brought to school in anticipation of this evening. Most stood in small groupings all along the water's edge. A few random couples could be seen sneaking off into the woods. Some kids were swimming in the river. I couldn't be sure from the distance, but it looked like at least one of the girls in the water was topless. Everyone—apart from those in the water—was holding red plastic party cups in their hands. A keg sat in a big plastic bucket full of ice not far from the bonfire. I nudged Quinn and pointed to it. "Want a drink?"

"I . . . sure." Quinn looked like he was turning a bit green at the thought of it. That made me chuckle.

"You don't drink, do you?" It was no big deal to me if he drank or not. I didn't, and I'd known plenty of people who didn't drink booze. In fact, back in Cali, my roommate Connor was straightedge. He didn't drink, didn't smoke, and didn't do drugs at all. I admired him for it. It was hard to stick to your ideals when most teenagers seemed to major in peer pressure.

"Not normally." I suspected that what he meant by "not normally" was "not ever," but some guys just couldn't lay it on the table when it came to experience and lack thereof.

"You don't have to drink. But people can be real dicks about the whole drinking or not drinking thing. So . . . I'll share my secret with you. Maybe it'll help you, maybe it won't." I directed him to the keg and filled two cups, handing him one. Mine had far more foam on top than his. "Ya see, the key to drinking at a party and not getting stupid wasted is to do what I do. Hold a cup, and sip from it every once in a while. You don't have to take big drinks. Hell, you don't even have to swallow. Just let the booze touch your lips enough to make it seem like you're drinking. As long as you have a cup in your hand, no one will pressure you to drink more. I think I've finished maybe half a beer at each of the First Nights I've been to."

Quinn blinked at me like I was the smartest man on earth. I wasn't. But I also didn't correct him. "That's actually pretty brilliant."

I shrugged. "I don't really like drinking. But I also don't

really like the bullshit peer pressure. It's an easy way to basically avoid both."

A guy I vaguely recognized let out a scream and ran over to a buddy of his, tackling him into the water. I'd never understood people like that—people who craved the spotlight, needed the attention to be on them for even a little while. I'd always stood on the sidelines, watching social interaction the way that one might observe a sociology experiment. I took mental notes on how people interacted, and questioned why they did. Grace used to say I was more like an alien than a human being for that reason. Maybe she was right.

"Any tips on how to talk to someone you're interested in?"

I followed Quinn's eyes to a familiar-looking girl who was seated all alone on a smooth log close to the river. Smiling both at the sight of her and at the idea that Quinn might be into her, I said, "Yeah. Start with 'hi.'"

As if the word *hello* were beyond his comprehension, Quinn froze. I patted him on the shoulder, told him I'd be right back, and then walked over to where the girl was sitting. As I took a seat beside her on the log, I said, "I thought you weren't coming tonight."

Caroline was staring at the water, but I got the feeling her mind was somewhere else. I got the impression that

Caroline's mind was almost always somewhere else. Without as much as a glance in my direction, she said, "Things change. Nature of the universe and all that."

I held my red plastic cup up for a moment. "Can I get you a beer?"

"I don't drink."

Why wasn't I surprised? "Can I introduce you to a few people?"

"Probably. But I'd rather you didn't." Her eyes never left the water. It was as if its movement mesmerized her. Either that or she was somewhere off on Planet Caroline.

I didn't mind her quirks. In fact, I found them more intriguing than I would admit to, if asked. "Well, can I at least hang out with you for a little while?"

"I guess. But I don't understand what you want to accomplish by doing so."

I shrugged. "I dunno. Conversation, maybe?"

"What do you want to talk about?"

"Anything. Just . . . whatever. The weather, why the sky is blue. I don't care. Just something." Talking to Caroline was like pulling teeth. And I didn't just mean that in the metaphorical way. Last year, we'd dissected a boar, but not just the organs and brain matter. We'd taken its bones apart and pulled out several teeth. It was a pain in the ass. But somehow intriguing. Like talking to Caroline.

"A prism." Just as I was about to inquire what the hell she was talking about, she continued. "Our atmosphere acts as a prism and bends the light of the sun into what we perceive as an array of colors. That's why the sky is blue."

She looked up at the night sky and sighed. "Not now, of course."

Surrendering to my frustration, I gestured to Quinn, who was still in the same spot where I'd left him. Only now he was shuffling his feet and looking up at the trees. "See that guy over there? The one looking a little awkward and alone? The one by the keg pretending to drink that beer?"

Her eyes followed my line of sight.

"Yeah. What about him?"

"His name's Quinn. He's my roommate. It's his first year at Wills, and I think you guys might get along. You should go say hi to him."

For a moment, she didn't move. Then, without a word, she stood up and walked over to Quinn. Quinn's face was a mixture of beet red and nausea green. I got the feeling he didn't talk to a lot of girls on his own. Especially ones he found interesting.

After a moment, Caroline walked away, down the trail that led back to the dorms. Once she was gone, I headed back to Quinn. "So? What did she say?"

"She just said hi. That was it." He tilted his cup up and

took an extremely healthy swallow. Something told me Quinn wasn't grasping the notion of just pretending to drink so you could keep your wits about you. Or maybe he really did want to get drunk. After he swallowed, he wiped his mouth off on the back of his hand and said, "Then she walked away."

I couldn't even pretend that I was surprised. "Caroline's . . . a little different. You should get to know her though. She seems nice."

"I knew you'd be here, ya liar." A familiar arm wrapped around my neck and squeezed in a playful headlock. As Josh released my head, I shoved him lightly, a grin spreading across my face. With his arm still around my shoulders, he looked at Quinn and smiled. "Who's this? The new roomie?"

The party had already improved by leaps and bounds now that Josh was here. The music was the same; the fire and teenage debauchery hadn't escalated at all. But just knowing my best friend was around somehow made it all feel a little different, better. "Yes, we're roomies. Quinn, this pain in the ass is Josh. Contrary to the things I'll be telling you about him later, he's a good guy."

"Nice to meet you." Quinn shook Josh's hand. As he let go, his eyes fell on someone behind me. "Oh . . ."

Josh and I both turned, watching as Grace settled onto the ground beside the fire pit. He and I exchanged looks that said we were both thinking the same thing—this ought to be interesting.

Quinn was oblivious to the fact that he was drooling over my sister, despite my warnings the previous day. To be fair, he was already halfway through his third beer. As we gravitated away from the keg, he slurred, "She's seriously hot."

As Quinn slurred the word *seriously*, Josh raised his eyebrows and took a sip from his own cup. I could tell he was amused, and I just wanted to watch the whole thing play itself out. With a smirk, I said, "Ya think so, eh?"

"Yeah. Do you know her?"

"You might say that." I waited until he'd brought his cup away from his mouth and met my eyes. Then I said, "That's my sister. Grace. Remember? From the dining hall?"

"Grace . . ." Quinn's eyes widened and I began to wonder how a guy like that had been admitted to Wills. "Oh! Oh, dude, I'm sorry. I didn't realize that was your sister. She looks different at night."

Josh laughed, coughing up a mouthful of beer. He was enjoying this more than he should have been.

I said, "That's because it's dark. And you're drunk."

Quinn grabbed my shoulder a little too firmly and breathed into my face, "I am *so* sorry."

I took a step back in search of fresh air. "It's cool, man. No big deal. Lots of guys like Grace. But Grace has never really liked anyone for very long."

Quinn wavered slightly and then turned back to the keg. When he spoke, it didn't seem to be to Josh or me. Maybe he was talking to the brain cells he was destroying. "I'm gonna get more beer."

As soon as he'd gone, Josh wiped a spot of beer Quinn had spilled on him, then turned to look at me. His expression went from smiling to serious—more serious than First Night generally called for. "Hey, Adrien, listen. I'm really glad you came tonight. Cuz I've gotta tell you something."

I raised a smartass eyebrow at him. "Is it bad? Should I actually start drinking this beer?"

"Maybe. I'm not sure how you'll react." He looked at my cup and bit his bottom lip for a moment before speaking again. "On second thought, maybe you should be sober for this."

I placed my hand on his shoulder and squeezed. "What is it, Josh? You know you can tell me anything."

His face was flushed, despite the fact that he seemed dead sober. When he met my eyes, he looked more than a little concerned. "It's . . . it's about Grace, kinda. I didn't say anything earlier, because I was really surprised to see you back at Wills and all. But . . . well . . . Grace and I sorta dated all last year."

I bit the inside of my cheek. Hard. "Is that right?"

Josh shrugged, guilt written all over his face. "I would have said something right away, but at least I'm saying it now before you hear it from somebody else."

Cutting the guy a break, I slapped him on the shoulder. We'd been friends for too long to have someone like Grace come between us. "It's okay, man. She dumped you. It's over. You should've told me. But it's cool. Whatever."

"Actually, I dumped her. She was pretty hurt over the whole thing. But I had my reasons." He cringed. "Gonna kick my ass?"

Laughter boiled out of me. "Kick your ass? For breaking Grace's heart? My friend, I'm going to buy you a drink."

Josh returned to the keg, refilled his cup, and took a healthy sip. I walked over to him and waited. When he looked at me again, he said, "I didn't mean to hurt her. Grace is just . . . I dunno. Not right for me, y'know?"

"Dude, Grace isn't right for a Minotaur. She's too much of an evil beast." I couldn't contain a chuckle. "I must confess, I'm feeling a bit smug over the idea of my best friend breaking her heart. Does that make me a cold bastard?"

Josh grinned. "The coldest. But screw it. We're young. Now's the time for mistakes and heartbreaks."

A couple of guys were taking turns jumping over the bonfire. The last one to do so, some kid I didn't recognize, caught his sneaker on fire. He stomped it out before the flames could reach his socks, but it was a pretty clear indication that it was almost time for me to leave. In my experience, once drunk people started setting themselves on fire, the party was pretty much over.

A couple of people I didn't know called Josh over to settle an argument over who was a better band—Greek Fire or Mindless Self Indulgence, which was like comparing apples to oranges or one great band to another. Senseless.

"I don't give a damn! Just do it, Marissa, before I rip your pretty hair out of your pretty little head."

Swerving my head toward my sister's voice, I saw her jabbing a girl in the shoulder with a perfectly manicured fingernail. The girl's face was drawn and tight in a way that suggested she was royally pissed off, but not about to argue with the queen. Her only response to my sister before stomping away was a single word, gritted through her clenched teeth. "Fine."

Once she'd gone, I couldn't resist seizing the moment to go stand beside my sister. "So I just heard you dated Josh last year."

"I thought we had a deal you were going to leave me alone," she said. When I continued to stand there with a satisfied grin on my face, she said, "If you must know, yes, I did." She glared at me, but her expression softened when she found Josh in the crowd. "Did he say anything about me?"

"Just that you were a terrible kisser. The worst he's ever had, actually." I took a sip of my beer, my lips curling into a smile behind the cup.

She groaned and faced me directly. "Why do you have to be such a prick, Adrien? Seriously. Why can't you just pretend to be decent?"

I shook my head, feigning innocence and ignorance. "So I'm not supposed to be bothered by the fact that you were screwing my best friend?"

She tilted her head to one side, eyeing me with pure hatred. "Shouldn't you be more bothered by the fact that your best friend screwed your sister?"

"Believe me, Grace, I'm more bothered by that than I can even put into words." Her eyebrows wrinkled in confusion. "I thought my friends had better taste than that."

She rolled her eyes. "You're such a virgin."

True or not, I never got why that was an insult. It was just another state of being.

My jaw flexed in irritation. "Look, just stay away from all of my friends, okay?"

As I turned to leave, she called after me, "Shouldn't be difficult. You have so few."

I yelled back, "Now who's being a prick?"

Josh rejoined me at the keg, where it seemed that our good friend Quinn had made it his duty to empty the damn thing. "What'd your sister have to say?"

I shook my head. "Nothing good about you, my friend. Nothing good at all."

His eyes followed her as she disappeared into the darkness of the woods, and I immediately recoiled. All he said was, "Huh." But I could tell by the look on his face that I'd planted a seed of curiosity where I'd hoped to poison the soil. Damn.

Maybe Grace was right. Maybe I was a prick.

Quinn grabbed me by the shirt and said, "I think I might be drunk."

Then he threw up.

On my shoes.

CHAPTER 7

HUND'S RULE:

Electrons are most stable if they remain unpaired in the ground state

"Tie, Mr. Dane."

I rolled my eyes as I straightened my tie, tightening it around my neck, as required by the uniform handbook. But the moment Mr. Garrow—a teacher who'd never cared much for either of my parents—was out of sight, I loosened it again, pulling it slightly to the side. I'd never understood boarding schools' anal need for dress conformity. What we wore didn't matter, and such limiting rules were enough to suck the creative juice out of every student here. Several years ago, I'd questioned the headmaster about the strict dress code at Wills. In response, he'd cited that Albert Einstein wore the same outfit every day so that he didn't have to waste any of his thinking on what to wear. The headmaster had had a point, but that still didn't mean I was going to conform to their rules. Even after that conversation, I continued to wear Chucks instead of polished black oxfords. No one cared about my footwear. So why did Mr. Garrow seem to give such an enormous crap about my tie?

I walked up to the door of Julian's class and took a deep breath. By some miracle, it turned out this was the only class I'd have with Grace, and even better, it was only twice a week. Eight classes. Then it was back to California and the life I'd built far away from my sister.

I opened the door, feigning confidence, and swept the room quickly with my eyes before I took a seat by the window, knowing that from a psychological standpoint I was saying that I was perfectly comfortable in this room, in this situation. I relaxed in my chair, trying to come across as blasé, but the truth was, I'd seen the roster for this class. Josh and Quinn—my only friends here, if you didn't count Caroline—weren't in this class. Just Grace, and everyone who hung out with Grace. To say I was feeling a little unnerved was an understatement. I was counting on Julian to keep the tension as low as possible. As he walked in, he smiled at me, easing my nerves some. The room filled, with Grace entering last. We sat on opposite sides of the room. I wasn't the least bit surprised.

Julian stood at the front of the class, tall and confident, clearly eager to set a good impression during his first week of classes as a teacher at Wills. His tie was perfectly straight, his oxfords polished to a shine—despite the fact that the teachers' dress code wasn't as strict as the students'. "Welcome to communication. This class has been arranged to educate you on something that many people struggle with and to ease your way into the world, wherever life may take you after graduation. It was also designed to help you before then. From what I hear, a lot of you at Wills seem content to study at all hours and spend most of your time in your rooms. The administration hopes to change this—to empower you to make a community here. The tools that you will learn in this class are invaluable. Together we will explore how to break down barriers and connect with others, despite the challenges we might face. It will be eye-opening, I'm sure. My name is Mr. Smith, but to start things off right and equalize us all, I'd like you all to call me Julian."

Julian looked nervous. I doubted that anyone else could tell, but I knew him. He was fiddling with his wedding ring and darting his eyes from one student to the next. I wondered how long he'd practiced his spiel in the mirror. If my classmates noticed, they didn't show it. They merely sat in silence.

Julian slapped his hands together to break the tension, flashing us all that Julian smile—the one you wanted to trust, even if you were hesitant to. "First off, I want you to move your chairs into a circle. We each have an equal voice in our discussions and I want to make sure that all of your voices are heard. After that, we'll discuss our class objective in detail."

As everyone stood and began shifting their chairs around, I remained where I was, locking eyes with Julian. I held my hands palms up in a question. *What the hell, Julian? Seriously.* Were we in elementary school and this was sharing time?

But Julian merely pointed to my chair and then to the empty spot left in the broken circle. Reluctantly, I picked up my chair and moved it into the place intended for me. Immediately, the girl to my left and the boy to my right slid their chairs several inches away, like I had some kind of disease or something. This was so childish. The next thing you knew, he'd be dividing us up into groups.

"Every day we'll participate in group discussions and group activities, but seventy percent of your grade will be dependent on a single project—one which you will complete together. In groups of two."

A pinprick headache formed quickly above my left eyebrow. I knew what was coming, and I knew that Viktor must have had a hand in it. I didn't have to look across the room to know that Grace was feeling the same way. Golly gee, I wondered who I'd be working with.

Julian began reading off names in pairs, moving down the list until he came to the one I'd been waiting to hear. "Grace Dane?"

I glanced over at my sister, who was looking at Julian stone-faced. For a second, I saw our mother in her profile. My heart softened in a moment of mourning at the hint of the woman who had soothed my nightmares and bandaged my wounds, but it didn't last. I refused to let it. Grace was nothing like our mother. Still I watched her, wondering what cracks would form in her expression when Julian spoke my name. Surely, she had to know it was coming.

"You'll be paired with Marissa Connelly."

Relief filled Grace's features. Confusion must have filled mine. I'd been pretty well convinced that I'd had it all figured out, that Julian was planning to use this class project as a way to bond my sister and me together somehow. The notion that I'd been wrong shook me slightly. But the shock didn't last long. Good. I still wanted to know what she was up to, but I didn't think being joined at the hip for the next month was the best way to achieve that.

A girl sitting three chairs to my right said, "Marissa's out. Apparently there was a mix-up at the chemistry lab this morning and she had to be taken to the hospital. They think it might be cyanide poisoning."

Marissa. Marissa. The name sounded familiar. And then it hit me—the girl Grace had been arguing with at the party last night.

"Jesus." The word left my mouth without thought. Everyone looked at me for a moment before returning their collective attention back to our instructor.

"That's terrible. I hope the rest of you will be that much more careful around all those chemicals. I heard Mr. Meadows has you trying to blow up furniture, first thing in the school year? Even one mislabeled bottle can do so much damage." Julian shook his head. I wondered how far my parents were from his thoughts. "Ah, well. Moving on. Let's see . . . ah. Grace, it looks like you'll be partnering with Adrien instead."

Of course.

My tension returned, but as I glanced back at Grace, I noticed her tension had intensified as well, and I took a small amount of satisfaction in that. Looking on the bright side, I realized that spending more time with Grace might lead me to the answers about her involvement in what happened to our parents. The best place to begin was at her side.

Grace raised her hand, and when Julian nodded at her, she said, "Exactly what will this partner project entail?"

"I was just about to get to that." Julian turned to the smart board and began typing out bulleted points on his laptop, which then appeared on the board. "Each member of the partnership will be responsible for creating an extensive case study on the other member. I want you to learn their background, what you think are the major influences in their life, and what you'd say is their preferred method of communication. Ultimately, I want you each to tell me in thirty pages why your partner communicates in the way that they do, and how best to reach them in a way that will encourage them to effectively and freely communicate."

I snorted. "Sounds more like social psychology than communication."

Julian locked eyes with me. "You don't consider the two linked, Mr. Dane?"

"I don't consider them at all, actually. As I'm sure you know, I prefer the actual sciences."

"Thank you, Mr. Dane, for demonstrating why this class has been put on the list of electives here at the Wills Institute." A girl seated across from me chuckled. A guy near her laughed and then coughed into his hand. To my right, someone snorted. Julian retrieved a stack of paper packets from his desk and began passing them around the circle of roughly twenty students. Each packet looked to be about five pages thick, presumably his class syllabus and further, detailed instructions for our ridiculous partnered project. As he passed one to me, he said, "Seems like you have a lot to learn . . . particularly about communication."

It was strange, my return to Wills. When I'd left, I wasn't popular, but I was well liked by most everyone—staff and students alike. And now I was a joke, a pariah, and an arrogant dickweed who had abandoned his sister in her time of mourning. *Her* time. As if I were not allowed to have had my own. And now even Julian was joining their chorus of dissent.

Not that I was wallowing in self-pity or anything.

Inside my pants pocket, my phone buzzed. No one heard it, but if I were caught with it on, I'd get a demerit and assigned chores. I was mad enough at Julian that I almost didn't care. But then Julian got a phone message of his own and stepped into the hall for a moment to check it, giving me the chance to pull out my phone and look at it. As I'd suspected, the unknown number from before had texted again. **Where does she go at night?**

I held the phone out of sight and texted back. **Who is this?**

What does she do there? What is she hiding?

Answer me, asshole. For the last time, who is this?

Watch her. Tonight.

"Adrien." Julian stepped back into the room, looking

less than pleased with me. "You know the rules."

"Come on, Julian. Give me a break."

He looked at my phone, disappointment filling his eyes. "Hand it over and report to the headmaster. And just so you know, I want you and Grace to focus your background research largely on the past four years you've spent apart."

I stood up and slapped my phone into his palm before walking out the door. I'd agreed to take Julian's class to help him out, so he'd have a familiar face in the crowd, somebody to have his back in case things got sticky. But now he was just being a dick to me. And why? To prove a point? And exactly what was the point, anyway?

I ambled down the hall and knocked on Headmaster Snelgrove's door. He opened it, looking surprised to see me. "Adrien Dane. To what do I owe the pleasure of your company so very early in the semester?"

"Jul—Mr. Smith sent me here for using my cell phone during class." It was impossible to keep the bitterness out of my voice.

"Not a wise way to begin your senior year, now is it? You know the rules." He took his seat behind his desk and gestured for me to sit down across from him. "One demerit. You'll spend an hour assisting our custodial staff after class tomorrow. Now, why don't we have a little chat?"

Reluctantly, I took a seat, sighing. "Awesome."

The headmaster met my eyes, his expression warm. I'd known him for as long as I'd been attending Wills. He was a kind man, and fair, but firm. Of the staff here that weren't family to me, he was probably my favorite, if I'd been asked to choose. It didn't hurt that he and my dad had been very close. "How are you, Adrien? Adjusting okay? I've already heard a few things that have given me some concern."

I didn't know how much to tell him. It wasn't the Wills Institute that was making me miserable. It was Grace. It was me. It was my parents, my past, and the sick glue that stuck it all together. I shrugged as casually as I could manage, but it was clear he saw through my calm facade. "Nothing I can't handle. Mostly gossip and speculation and people taking sides where there are none to take."

He sat back in his chair, lacing his fingers together on his stomach. "I was happy to learn of your return to the Wills Institute. I hope it was your decision, and not something that you regret doing."

"Truthfully, I would have much rather stayed in California, and I plan on returning there in the next few weeks. Just have some things to sort out first. But I'm happy to be here. Everyone has been so warm and welcoming, it's almost as if I never left." Sarcasm practically dripped from every last syllable I spoke. Mostly because I was making no attempt to mask it. We both knew I didn't want to be here. Why pretend?

Headmaster Snelgrove tilted his chin into his chest and eyed me over his glasses. "I understand that your godfather asked you to return. Sort of a personal favor."

"He did. It's fine. I just . . . I have some things to work out and then I'm sure the rest of my time here will be smooth." It was a lie, and we both knew it. I wasn't sure of anything, and I wasn't happy to be back. It was nothing against the school. But the Wills Institute was my past, and I had left it a long time ago. I cleared my throat against my fist. "Can I go now?"

He looked at me as if gauging my potential reaction to what he was about to say. Then he offered up a thin-lipped frown. "We have a wonderful new counselor on staff. Perhaps you'd consider stopping in and saying hello?"

"Yeah, maybe." Another lie. Apparently, I was full of them. Speaking of being full of things, I'd also already had my fill of counseling, thank you very much.

"I'll let you get back to class now. And Mr. Dane . . ." He sat forward, raising his eyebrows at me. "Rules are in place for a reason. Please try to remember that."

I stood without another word and exited his office. As I walked out the door, Mr. Garrow passed by and said, "Tie, Mr. Dane."

I muttered, "Screw your tie."

He whipped around to face me, his eyes wide at what he

thought he'd heard. "Excuse me?"

I blinked at him, then smiled politely, adjusting my tie. "I just said I needed a new tie. This one doesn't like to hold its knot."

He narrowed his gaze at me—not entirely certain he'd misheard me the first time. "Get back to class."

"Yes, sir." As I turned away from him, I loosened my tie again and headed to Julian's classroom.

I opened the door, and whatever discussion had been going on ceased. I held my hand out to Julian, my jaw clenched. "I'm here for my phone."

The look in his eyes was pleading with me to just calm down and realize that he was in the right here. But I was too far beyond pissed for that now. It was bad enough that the entire school was against me. But Julian? That was too much.

He handed me my phone with an air of reluctance, and then I picked up my books and moved out the door. His voice followed me into the hall. "Adrien—"

"Nope." The door clicked shut to punctuate my response. As I moved down the hall, I thumbed through the school directory site on my phone until I found Marissa's father's number.

Clicking the number, I put the phone to my ear. It rang twice before a man answered. "Hello?"

"Yes, Mr. Connelly? My name is Adrien Dane. I go to school with Marissa here at Wills and just heard about her condition. I wanted to make sure she's okay."

His voice sounded rough, jagged with worry. "Nice of you to call, Adrien. Marissa's . . . she's not great. I'm afraid she won't be returning to school anytime soon. And frankly, after what happened this morning, I'm not sure she'll be returning to Wills when she does."

"I'm so sorry to hear that. Do . . ." I hesitated, choosing my words carefully. "Do they know what caused it?"

His voice shook when he spoke. "It was an accident. A bizarre one that should never have been allowed to happen on a school campus, but an accident all the same."

An accident. Right. One caused by a certain angry friend by the name of Grace Dane. "Please tell her I hope she feels better soon."

"I will. Thanks for calling." The call ended and I started to climb the tower stairs. I didn't stop moving until I came to my door. Written on it in Sharpie in big, bold letters was the word *traitor*. I stood there staring at it for a good, long time. Is that what I was? A traitor? To whom? Grace? The Wills Institute? The entire student population? Had I committed some grievous offense, some unforgivable sin by leaving behind my parents' deaths and a sister who hated me and trying to find my own way to deal with my grief? I'd dealt with my grief by leaving it behind. Why the hell was that a problem, or anyone else's business for that matter?

I opened the door to my room, slamming it behind me. I could have called the resident advisor and reported the graffiti, but screw it. Screw them. If this was how the student body wanted to view me, then fine. I was a traitor. Hell, Benedict Arnold was a traitor here in the states, but a hero in England. He even got a statue. Maybe I'd get a statue, too. It just wouldn't be at the Wills Institute. Besides, my time here was quickly shrinking. So was Viktor's. After that, I was gone. Outta here. Never looking back.

I lay on my bed for the rest of the day, watching as the light moved down the walls to the floor before disappearing altogether. My mind was filled with more noise than anything, swirling thoughts of what to do and what I had done, analyzing and overanalyzing and coming up empty-handed. When it got too dark to see without turning on the light, I left my room and went to see Josh at the radio station.

When I got there, he looked at me with a half smile, half frown that said he'd already heard about what had happened in Julian's class. "Ahh, if it isn't Mr. Popularity."

"Bite me." I sat on the couch, placing my face in my palms with a heavy sigh. "How do I fix this, Josh? I've never been a good student, but I used to love being at this school. Now I'm a social pariah. It's beyond stupid."

"You're not who you were when you were here before, Dane. You're a different guy, with a different life. You can't expect to walk in and resume your old life when you haven't been here to live it." "Losing Sleep" by John Newman came to an end. Josh turned in his chair and flipped a couple of switches, not taking time to say anything into the microphone. "Swing Life Away" by Rise Against started to play. Josh turned back to face me. "Grace stayed. So while her life is different, too, the whole school has watched that change in her. No one knows the changes in you. So of course they side with her."

He crossed his arms in front of his chest and leaned back in his chair. It sounded like he'd given this entire situation a lot of thought. It was comforting to know that I wasn't alone in that, anyway. "It may sound stupid, but if you want to fix this and have a relatively pleasant time here, I'd recommend getting involved. Be seen at the parties, let shit go when people attack you. Laugh it off, even if you don't feel like it. Basically don't be a dick. And don't let them push you out."

I shook my head, dropping my hands in my lap. "I'm not kissing ass just to get accepted."

He stood up from his chair and took a seat beside me on the couch, giving me a friendly pat on the knee. "I'm not saying you should kiss anyone's ass. I'm saying that you have this wall around you that's made of solid, four-foot-thick 'screw you,' and if you don't knock it down, you're going to have a very lonely time here."

A hundred defensive thoughts ran through my mind—most prominently "screw you," which only served to prove that he was right. I took a deep breath and blew the thoughts away in an attempt to take Josh's advice. When I looked at him, I simply said, "Okay."

He raised an eyebrow at me. "Okay?"

"Where do I start?"

A smile touched his lips. "There's a small party in the art barn on Friday. Just a dozen or so people. Come with me, maybe smile at a few people, hold your tongue once in a while, and we'll see what happens."

He hesitated a moment before he said, "Grace will be there. But if you want everyone to stop hating you, you've gotta learn to be in the same room with her. Without that angry wrinkle permanently creasing your forehead."

Josh was right. I knew he was right, but hated that he was. We both stood and I grabbed his hand after we high fived, pulling him into a hug. I said, "Thanks, man."

As we parted, he said, "No problem. That's what friends are for . . . right?"

I walked out of the room, feeling lighter and heavier at the same time.

As I reached the ground floor of the library, I caught a glimpse of Grace as the back door closed behind her. It wasn't like her to be by herself at night. She should have been hanging out with her friends in the common room or at the dining room holding court after dinner. She was up to something, and it was about damn time I found out what.

She didn't see me, and I waited a moment before following just to make sure it stayed that way. Then I opened the door and stepped outside, quietly closing it behind me. She was moving across the courtyard, her steps hurried and determined. I moved along the hedges beside the main building, hiding in the shadows. She stopped momentarily and pulled out her phone. Her thumbs moved over the glowing screen, but I couldn't tell what she was writing or even whether it was a text message or something else.

Before she started moving again, she looked around, as if suspecting that someone might be following her. I held my breath. Finally, she moved forward again and rounded the end of the building. I took two slow, deep breaths and followed her . . . but when I turned the corner, she was nowhere to be found. Whoever had been texting me was right again—Grace was sneaking around at night. Where was she going? What was she doing? And who else besides me had been following her?

CHAPTER 8

NONPOLAR COVALENT BOND:

A type of bond that occurs when two atoms
share a pair of electrons with each other

I closed my notebook and slid it inside my top drawer. I was no closer to turning any of my three hypotheses into theories, and here we were in the middle of the first week. Time was getting away from me faster than I liked.

Quinn rushed through the door in a whirlwind, grabbing his backpack from the back of his chair. I looked up at him to ask what the hurry was, but he cut me off with a breathy "I'm late!" before disappearing out the door once again. I was late, too, but I didn't think it mattered all that much. What was five minutes in the grand scheme of things?

Slipping my already-knotted tie over my head, I grabbed my books and headed out the door to the first class of the day. If I was honest with myself, I was kind of looking forward to it. But then, the idea of blowing anything up had always given me a delightfully tingly sensation at the base of my skull. Besides, Caroline had surprised me with her potassium suggestion . . . and I didn't often get surprised. In hindsight, I should have thought of it first. It was so obvious. But I hadn't. And she had. It made me wonder what else was rattling around in that head of hers—a curiosity I hadn't felt before about anyone else, whether male or female or whatever other gender someone identified as. She was unusual. And I liked unusual things.

Not that she was a thing.

The door was already closed by the time I approached Mr. Meadows's classroom. I knew it would likely mean another demerit to be late to class, but I was allowed ten before things got serious, and there was no way I was going to be at Wills long enough to use up all ten. Besides, like I gave a crap how red Meadows's face would get when he laid eyes on me. After the way he'd treated Caroline on the first day of class, I didn't mind bugging the crap out of him.

Mr. Garrow stopped me in the hall just long enough to snarl at me. He said, "Tie, Mr. Dane," just as I opened the door to the class, and all eyes turned to me. I moved slowly, confidently to my spot at the table beside Caroline and took a seat.

I pretended not to hear him. Who cared if my tie was tight and straight anyway? Besides Garrow, I mean. I was wearing it, which was all that the handbook demanded of me as far as the tie situation was concerned. I liked to think of my loose tie as a middle finger I wore around my neck. And it seemed like Garrow did, too—his offense felt like an acknowledgment that I had just metaphorically flipped him the bird.

"As I was saying before we were so rudely interrupted," Meadows—a hippie who likely sang along to tunes about peace, love, and harmony, I might remind you—continued, "I want each of your tests to be thoroughly documented both on paper and on film. Start small, people, and use the least amount of chemical interaction required to blow your bathtub to smithereens. Safety first. And each test requires the presence of a staff member. That being said, the remainder of your class time today will be active lab. If you have any questions at all, I am at your disposal . . . as are the materials in the supply closet. All chemicals must be approved for sign out. Other than that, as you are AP students, I trust your judgment."

I looked at Caroline and said, "So. Potassium."

"Potassium." She nodded. "I'll handle the paperwork, if

you don't mind. Documenting experiments has always been my strong suit. Equations? Not so much."

"Fine with me. I figured we could do any small tests on the soccer field. Less chance of damage to school property." My pause was one filled with uncertainty. "I hope."

"What should we blow up first?"

"I think we should listen to Meadows, start small. Coffee can?"

Caroline chewed on the end of her pencil for a moment before rolling her eyes. "Oh, come on. Let's at least use a trash can. Bigger is better, don't you think? Especially if our end goal is to destroy a bathtub."

A smile touched the corners of my mouth. I was pretty certain I liked Caroline. Anybody who thought bigger was better when it came to chemical reactions was all right in my book. "Trash can it is."

"Now we just need to calculate how much water and potassium we'll need."

"Slow your roll. First we need the dimensions of the trash can. Which means we're going to need to obtain a trash can. A metal one. We want something sturdy." I glanced at her notebook. "Are you taking notes?"

"Of course." She picked up her pencil and jotted down everything we'd discussed so far. The outside of her notebook was covered with stickers and random doodles. Mostly things like hearts and rainbows, but also an inked tribute to some band called Rancid.

An enigma. That's what Caroline was.

When she'd finished writing, I said, "So there's this party Friday—"

"Not interested."

"You don't have to drink or anything."

"No, I mean in you. I'm not interested." She looked at me briefly and shrugged. There was no feeling in it. Not even a tiny amount of regret. "In you. Sorry."

I blinked in wonder. Was I really so dull? Was the idea of hanging out with me for even a few hours so repulsive? Not to be arrogant or anything, but I thought I had some pretty interesting ideas about the way the world worked. And for the most part, I liked what I saw when I looked in the mirror. Well . . . maybe not first thing in the morning, but still. "Why?"

"Why am I sorry or why am I not interested?"

"Both, I suppose."

She set her pencil down and met my eyes. "I'm sorry because it's the polite thing to be when you turn someone down for a date. And I'm not interested in being an accessory to a great mind, when I have one of my own."

I shook my head, confused. And a little more than annoyed. "Yesterday you were questioning how you managed to get into AP Chemistry. Today you're a great mind?"

She shrugged and made an additional note on the page. "It's called experiencing a moment of self-doubt. Everyone does it on occasion."

Exasperated, I stumbled over my breath for a moment before speaking. "I just . . . don't understand. It's just a party. Could be fun."

"You don't want me to come have fun with you, Adrien. You want me to help you prove to people that you're not the jerk they all think you are." She bit the end of her pencil again and seemed to examine me before adding, "And I'm not yet convinced that you aren't."

I didn't know what to say to that. So I just sort of sat there, dumbfounded. Maybe I wasn't the only one forming hypotheses about the people around me.

I could understand how she might get the impression that I was some kind of jerk. But that wasn't the only reason I'd asked her to go with me. Honestly, I found her interesting. I just wasn't getting how she couldn't seem to reach that conclusion about me.

She went on as if nothing at all had happened. "We need a trash can. Maybe the kitchen staff can hook us up?"

Through a fog of hurt feelings, I muttered, "Yeah. Maybe. I'll ask at lunch."

"Good."

I leaned closer and said, "Let me get this straight. You're not attracted to me at all? Not even a little?"

"Honestly?"

"Honestly." She didn't even do me the courtesy of pausing to pretend she needed a moment to mull it over before she closed her notebook with a snap. On the front was a sticker that read *Luna Lovegood is my spirit animal.* She said, "I think you're attracted to yourself enough for the both of us."

After a long time filled with silence and note taking, the bell rang and my mood plummeted with its shrill sound. It wasn't like I was crazy attracted to Caroline or falling madly in love with her or anything. I just thought she was interesting. So where was the harm in spending more time together? And where would she get the impression that I was arrogant? Just because I generally liked myself and had confidence in my abilities meant that I was stuck-up? It was ridiculous. She was being completely unreasonable. This was one problem I was pretty sure even the scientific method couldn't help me understand. So maybe it was better that we didn't attend the party together after all.

The conversation with Caroline occupied my thoughts throughout the rest of the day, carrying me from one class to the next. I made halfhearted notes on each subject, and by the time I sat down in the circle in Julian's class, I was just ready for the day to be over.

Julian stood at the center of our circle, hands clasped behind his back. His tie was perfectly straight again today. I had the urge to loosen its knot and pull it off-center. He said, "What is communication?"

Grace raised her hand, and I suppressed a laugh at the notion that my sister had any real idea what communication was. "Communication is the exchange of thoughts, messages, or information, as by speech, signals, writing, or behavior."

Julian nodded. "A textbook definition, Grace. But at its core—what is communication?"

"The need to connect?" I didn't care if my answer was wrong. I just knew that that was what communication was to me—something that Grace and I had clearly never had between us.

Julian pointed at me with an approving gleam in his eyes. "Precisely. In this marvelous age of technology, communication is both changing forms and breaking down in many ways. While a new form of communication is born every day on the internet, other tried and true forms— languages, for instance—are slowly dying off. Did you know that there is a small village in Asia where the people used to communicate by whistling? Only about twelve people still know how to do it, where it used to be the primary form of conversation. Speaking of conversation, some might argue that the art of polite face-to-face conversation has even suffered across the globe in recent years. But at its essence, communication arises from the need to connect with our fellow human beings. A simple look, a touch, a word can express so much. It can unite humanity, or tear it apart completely. I want you to keep that in mind as we move forward in this class. The importance of communication in all its forms."

Communication was important. But part of communication was listening, and Grace and I had stopped listening to each other a long time ago.

For the first two years after I was adopted, I'd hung on Grace's every word. I'd wanted a sister who'd guide me and be my friend. Even from the start, she'd never seemed thrilled to have a brother, but at least she let me tag along. Then came the day that Scruffy died.

Scruffy was a mutt—a rather ugly dog that Dad had brought home against Mom's wishes when Grace and I were in the third grade. He was a sweet dog who loved to play catch. If it was a ball or a Frisbee, or anything ball- or Frisbee-shaped, and you threw it, Scruffy would go after it.

Grace and I would trade off who had to put Scruffy's toys away each day. Back then, we were pretty good about doing things like that without being told. But one evening, after a long day of running around outside, Grace reminded me that it was my turn to pick up Scruffy's toys. I told her I already had, but I hadn't. I was tired and just wanted to go inside. That night one of Scruffy's balls rolled out into the road. A truck hit him, and he died.

Grace never forgave me. I think from that day on, she felt like her worst fears were confirmed. She couldn't trust me. I wasn't a part of her family.

Julian seemed more confident today, or maybe he was just pleased with his approach to teaching. His mood seemed lighter than it had, that was for certain. "We'll begin preparation for your project by developing interview questions. Spend today developing fifty or so questions to ask your partner that will help you better understand their background. Write your questions down, but keep them to yourselves for now. On Tuesday, you'll begin interviewing one another. Now if you'll all switch seats so that you're seated by your partner . . ."

Grace and I exchanged looks. She wasn't going anywhere. As I begrudgingly took the seat next to her, I drew in a breath and said, "Let's just try to get through this without killing each other, shall we?"

The corner of her mouth twitched slightly. "That much I can manage. Depending on how much of an asshole you plan to be, that is."

Forcing a falsely charming smile, I set my notebook and pen on the desktop. "No more than the usual."

"Thanks for the warning." She sighed and immediately

went to scribbling down questions.

From out of the side of my eye, I watched her. It was the first time in four years that I had looked at her—really looked at her. And what I saw made my heart ache. Before I could catch myself, I said, "You look like her, y'know. More than I thought you would."

"Like who?" She didn't look up from her paper. Anything I had to say to her was less important than whatever she was writing. Or anything else in the world, for that matter.

"Mom."

She paused, loosening her grip on the pencil. Probably out of shock that I would admit such a thing. "Is that a compliment?"

I shrugged. It was. But there was no way I'd ever admit that to her. "Just an observation."

She kept staring at her paper, so it was hard to be sure, but I could swear I saw a glimmer of tears and remembrance in her eyes. In my mother's eyes. "Thank you."

I shrugged again, as if what I'd said had been nothing at all—maybe even just a joke. "Thank genetics. I had nothing to do with it."

We both went back to work in silence, the air strange and heavy between us. She had to be questioning my motives. The truth was, I didn't really understand why I'd said it. Maybe it was the shock of the moment. Maybe it was the ache that seeing those eyes had sent through me. I missed my mom. And it pained me that even a small part of her would live on forever in Grace. I had nothing from our parents— nothing tangible, nothing physical. I was just an abandoned boy, adopted by strangers and then abandoned again. Even with a sister, I was totally alone.

At the end of class, Julian called us up front. He sat on the corner of his desk, looking much more like the relaxed, casual Julian I knew outside of the classroom. "Viktor and I would love for you both to join us at a dinner party this Saturday. Adrien, our dinner parties tend to be relatively upscale, so please dress for the occasion."

Grace was first to respond. "You already know I'll be there. I told you yesterday."

Julian looked at me. "Adrien?"

"Yeah. Sure. Why not? It's not like I have other plans." I hadn't even finished my answer when Grace exited the room. Try as I might not to, I let my eyes follow her, wondering what life would have been like if Grace had been more open to having me in her family from the beginning. I'd never know for sure.

"Julian?" I met his eyes and hesitated before asking the question that was burning in my mind. "Do you ever get the feeling that Grace has her own agenda going on?"

Julian tilted his head at me curiously. "Don't we all?"

I bit the inside of my cheek, debating the possibility. "I suppose."

"Dinner's at eight o'clock Saturday. I'll send a cab. You won't have to share with Grace. She's getting a ride with a friend."

I nodded in response. I should have been more excited to see Viktor. Even if it meant having to get dressed up for a fancy dinner party, I was here, back at Wills, to spend as much time with Viktor as I could. But honestly, I couldn't give a crap. With a whole house full of guests to compete with there, I'd rather be doing just about anything else.

A smile settled on Julian's lips then. He knew how I felt about dressing up and impressing strangers. "Saturday. Eight o'clock. Wear a tie."

I didn't speak my response so much as sigh it. "See you then."

[CHAPTER 9]

MASS DEFECT:

*The difference between the mass
of the nucleus of an atom and the mass
of its constituent molecules*

The art barn had started out as a carriage house over a hundred years ago. The wood was all original, as were the large barn doors, but back in the 1920s the building had been converted to an art studio. All of the art classes at Wills—from painting to pottery to metalworking—were taught in or near this building. Inside on the walls hung proud examples of former students' work. Dangling from the ceiling were strings and strings of vintage Edison lights that emitted a soft, warm glow. "Action Cat" by Gerard Way greeted me as I entered the building. Someone had obviously hooked up an iPod to the barn's sound system. Only about a dozen or so people were there—and I was already getting tired of watching Josh stare longingly at the sliding barn door for any sign of my sister, despite the fact that I'd been in the building for only about five seconds or so. I sighed, reaching into the cooler for a can of Mountain Dew. "Well, this looks like a bust."

"It'll get better." Josh's tone was a mixture of nerves and determination. I was about to ask him where exactly he was hiding his crystal ball, but he interrupted my snark. "I asked your sister to meet me here."

I pinched the bridge of my nose and sighed. "Listen. Josh. Maybe this party was a bad idea. I think I'll just head back to the dorms."

The large door on the left slid open and Grace entered the barn. The moment she spotted Josh, she walked over. With a glance at me, she said to Josh, "And here I thought your taste in friends had improved."

Not exactly under my breath, I said, "And that's when the evening went completely to hell."

She tried to ignore me, but I could tell that my words had seeped through her stony exterior. Then her expression moved from annoyed with me to enamored with Josh in about two heartbeats. It was nauseating. "I can only stay for a few minutes. I got your note."

He said to her, "Can we talk? Somewhere private? It's important."

"Of course." She grabbed his hand and they began to walk away. Leaving me alone. At a party that I hadn't even wanted to attend.

"Josh?" He looked back at me, and I grabbed him by the arm, pulling him close and lowering my voice. "What are you doing?"

He shook his head, as if he wasn't really sure. "Just talking. Why?"

"I thought you broke up with her. What's there to talk about?"

"We did break up. Just . . . give me a minute, okay? I'll be right back." The look in his eyes had liar written all over it. He wasn't coming back and we both knew it.

As Grace tugged him across the room, I called after him, "And what exactly am I supposed to do until you get back?"

"Mingle?" It wasn't a suggestion so much as an off-chance possibility. Whatever Josh had to talk to Grace about, it had better be important. I wouldn't have come here if I'd known I was going to get ditched five seconds into my arrival.

"Mingle." The word dried up on my tongue, turning to ash. I rolled my eyes so far back in my head that I thought they might get stuck that way. Mingling wasn't exactly my strong suit. "Great."

I hopped up on a counter that doubled as a workspace and surveyed the crowd, sipping my soda and wishing I'd just stayed in my room. The crowd was still small, and I didn't really recognize any of the partygoers. But as I scanned the room, one set of eyes met mine. Casually, I continued my survey, but finally brought my attention back to her.

She was a pretty girl. No. That wasn't the right word at all. She was stunning. Flawless. Almost unreal. Like a walking fiction. Model hot. Tan and tall. Eyes like melted chocolate and hair to match. Her black dress clung to her thighs, her hips, her waist, her curves. I *definitely* didn't recognize her as someone I knew from before. A curious smile touched her lips as she approached the counter where I sat, as if we had business to attend to that I was not yet aware of. "Hi there."

"Well, hello." Smooth, Dane. Real smooth. "And to whom do I have the pleasure of speaking?"

What was I? A butler or something? I was starting to sound like Viktor. Not that he was a butler or anything, but he did have this old-man formality about him sometimes. Not that he was old. Or that I was old.

I was having a hard time focusing on words. Her legs were just that flawless.

"Charity Bernhart."

"Ahh. Of the Connecticut Bernharts." I nodded, lifting the left side of my mouth in what I hoped was a charming smirk.

She cocked an eyebrow and smiled. "You know my family?"

Blinking, I stumbled over my words. This whole charming thing was just not working out for me this week. It had always gone over fine in California. "No. I . . . made it up . . . actually. I don't know anyone here. Not really. Except Josh. But he's . . ."

I looked around, but Josh and Grace were noticeably absent. My imagination forced an image of them making out against a tree or something. Gross. ". . . somewhere."

"So you're Grace's brother, right?" Charity ran a well-manicured finger along my collar, tugging it slightly. "Adrien?"

Was it warm in here? It felt warm in here. "That I am. Not by blood, but still."

"Word has it you're quite the arrogant bastard."

I raised a sharp eyebrow. Silently, I wondered both who'd been saying that about me . . . and how right they might be. Maybe I was arrogant. Maybe that was exactly my problem. But I thought it was more likely something Grace had said before even getting to know the person I'd become.

She licked her lips then and met my eyes. "Fortunately for you, I'm into arrogant bastards."

"That's . . . good, I suppose?" It came out as a question. Mostly because I thought it was kind of a stupid thing to say to someone, but didn't want to insult her by saying so.

First off, my apparent arrogance all depended on who you asked, and we hadn't really been talking long enough for her to make that determination one way or another. Second, I detested the word *bastard*. I'd had two fathers—one by birth, one by adoption—and now I had none. So what gave anyone the right to call me by such a vile name?

I was beginning to hate how attracted I was to her.

She ran her finger up my collar again, over my chin to my bottom lip. A chill went through me, but I couldn't be certain if it was disgust or desire. "Wanna go for a walk?"

I swallowed hard and tried to keep my cool. "Where?"

Shrugging, she smiled. Not a happy smile or an act of pleasantry. But something deeper, darker—a smile of pure, animalistic intent. "Does it matter?"

I didn't have time to ponder whether it did or didn't, and frankly, I was beginning to care less about what my brain had to say about the matter. Before I could trip over any more words, she tugged me gently out the door. My collar in her hands, tugging me along in the dark. Me following her lead, letting myself be drawn into the unknown possibility of it all.

We walked away from the barn without talking. At one point, she let go of my shirt and laced her fingers with mine. At her insistence, we moved down the slope of a nearby hill, immersing ourselves in the night. The grass was covered in dew, as was the tree trunk I leaned against when we stopped walking. She moved closer to me—so close that I could feel her hot breath on my neck. And when she spoke, tiny goose bumps raised on my skin. "Has anyone ever told you how hot you are, Adrien?"

I wasn't sure she wanted an answer, or even what I'd say. But I didn't have time to form a response. Before I could, she pressed her curves to me, tangling her fingers in my hair, slipping her tongue inside my mouth. It was fast. Too fast. Suddenly the same pull that had led me out the door and down the hill tugged me out of the wave of desire with a warning. Did I want this—whatever it was? What kind of girl just grabs someone she's never met and takes them outside to screw around? Not that it was necessarily a bad thing, just a bold move that I wasn't quite used to experiencing. As turned on as I was, a strange sort of terror filled me. I didn't know if I wanted this. But more than that, I didn't know if it was okay to not want this.

Almost out of instinct, I pushed her gently away and said, "Whoa. Slow down. I think I'd rather talk for a while, if you don't mind."

She blinked at me and took a slow step back, as if drowning in disbelief. The sight of her grappling with rejection made me feel sorry for her. She was pretty, and probably a very bright person to be at Wills in the first place, but all her worth seemed tangled up in the physical affection she could offer. It made me wonder what her relationships with the men in her life were like. Did she have a bad relationship with her father? Her uncles? Her brothers? Were there no men in her life she could relate to? Was she seeking that connection by kissing strange guys in the dark? She raised an eyebrow at me in disbelief, as if I might be joking, as if no one had ever said no to her before. "Really?"

Even in the shadows, I could see that she was interpreting my offer to talk as a solid rejection. And this was not a girl used to being rejected. It occurred to me then that I didn't even know her name. She'd said it, but in that moment, suddenly, I couldn't recall it. Like a whisper on the wind—present, but easily forgotten. My chest tightened in panic. How could I not recall her name? I'd had it. It was just there. Catherine? Sharon?

I felt bad for my momentary lapse in memory. She deserved more than that. All girls did. All people did. "Yeah, really."

"I heard that about you," she said with an eye roll. There was a decided shift in her posture, her mood. Now I was an annoyance, no longer a prize. If I ever had been that.

"Heard what?" The noise from the party sounded so far away, despite the fact that the barn was merely yards up the hill from where we stood.

She started fixing her hair, even though it didn't need fixing at all. Nervous fidgeting, maybe. Then she snorted, her beauty immediately marred by her shift in attitude. "That you're asexual. Or gay. Or something. Gorgeous, but untouchable. Or maybe just afraid of losing your virginity?"

If there was one word that got my hackles up more than *bastard*, it was when people used *virgin* as an insult. As if we all hadn't been virgins at one point in time. As if virginity were some sort of sideshow attraction—something to be stared at in abject horror and wonder. Something that had existed eons before, but was completely extinct in this day and age.

"Who said I was a virgin? And what would it matter if I were?" I swallowed hard, gasping for air in a moment where I felt the need to defend myself—despite my belief that defense shouldn't be needed. "Not that I am."

"That's not what I heard."

And that's when I realized what this was. A total setup, likely by Grace. But what was the point? Did she really think being teased by some girl I'd just met would hurt me so terribly? Clearly my sister had a lot to learn about vengeance.

A cool breeze rustled the leaves above us. I'd forgotten how cold it could get here at night, and I still hadn't received the rest of my clothes and stuff from California. One week in, but already it felt like my real life was becoming more and more of a memory. I knew then that it was time to uncover what Grace had been up to with my father's work, say my good-byes to Viktor, and get back to California. Wills wasn't home. It was the shadow of a memory that belonged to someone else, and it would look a lot better in my rearview mirror.

She shook her head and sighed. "I knew it. I knew you were gay. Or some kind of asexual freak."

I looked at her, tilting my head to the side in a question. "So. Wait. Because I won't kiss you before getting to know you, I must only be attracted to the same gender or not interested in sex at all? Wow. Now who's being arrogant?"

She stared at me, mouth agape. I could only shrug.

The line of her mouth thinned with an air of cruelty. "So which is it? Are you queer or a prude?"

My jaw tightened. "My personal life, my orientation, the choices I make, and the genetics I'm predisposed to are none of your damn business. And I think this conversation has reached its conclusion."

"Fine by me." She moved back up the hill and I followed her with my eyes. As she reached the top, she called out, "He's all yours, boys."

At first, I had no idea what she was talking about or who she was talking to. But then three shapes stepped out from behind the surrounding trees, and I knew that I was in trouble. I recognized two of them—Carter Danvers and Taylor Watson, both athletes and constant occupants of the same lunch table where Grace had sat every day this week. I couldn't make out the third guy in the dark. But I knew trouble when I saw it. And he was definitely trouble.

I made a break for it, but Carter grabbed me by the arm and swung me back down the hill. Taylor grabbed my other arm, and their grips tightened. To my credit, I didn't cry out or plead for help—at first. But I couldn't hold my tongue as the third guy came down the hill—a guy I now thought I recognized as Ben Winchester from chemistry class. Try as I did to keep calm, my voice shook when I spoke. "Come on, guys. I already told her I don't feel like making out tonight. That includes with you."

The first punch hit my nose and I thought my head was going to explode. Tears rolled from my eyes. My entire face grew hot, and my nose throbbed in pain. If that hit had been the last of it, I would have happily agreed not to mess with Charity again.

Charity. That was her name. The punch in the face had apparently jogged my memory.

But as the hits kept coming, setting my jaw, my eye socket, my cheek alight with pain, I felt surer than ever that this little encounter wasn't about the girl at all. It was a setup. By Grace. Hell, maybe by Josh. Maybe both. Somebody had wanted to get me here all along and beat the crap out of me. Charity had just been the bait.

Could Josh really have been part of this? He had seemed anxious to see Grace tonight, and hurried off with her the moment she appeared. Had he been helping her? Was he merely another pawn in whatever game she had been orchestrating against me in my absence? He had insisted that I come tonight, after all. The hypothesis had a lot of evidence to support it.

I hung there between Carter and Taylor, barely able to keep myself upright. And finally, when Taylor let go and retreated back up the hill, I allowed myself a moment to think that it was over. Driving home the point that it wasn't, Carter punched me in the side, I fell with a groan, and Ben gave me a swift kick in the ribs. I lay there on the cool ground, in the darkness, feeling my entire body throb with pain, wondering what I had done that had deserved such a sharp retaliation. Slowly, with their laughter echoing behind them, my attackers left me alone in the woods.

I didn't move for a long time. I stayed there on the ground, listening to my heart race, my head pound. I tried not to cry, but tears pooled in my eyes and rained down the sides of my face, wetting my hair. Maybe it was stupid, maybe it was childish, and I'd never admit it to anyone if they asked—but in that moment, all I wanted was my mother.

Not that she'd been the most warm or loving parent. My mom had always been enveloped in her work and a huge supporter of independence in her children. But what I'd always wanted her to be was what I closed my eyes and wished for as I lay there on the ground. Her hand brushing the dirt and leaves from my hair. Her kiss on my brow. Her kind words telling me that everything would be all right.

What I wanted was a mother whom I had never known. A mother I would never have.

I rolled to the side and pushed myself up on my elbow, struggling to stand. Finally, I got to my feet, then moved up the hill, drying my tears with my sleeve. I headed straight back to my dorm without stopping, cradling my ribs and wincing with every step.

When I opened the door to my room, Quinn's eyes widened in shock. "Jesus, what happened to you?"

He helped me to my bed, where I sat with a groan. Deadpan, I said, "I went on a lovely Sunday picnic with twenty of my closest friends. We played croquet and badminton. It was nice."

"Did you get in a fight?" It was such an obvious statement that I wanted to laugh, but didn't, for fear of the pain.

"Not exactly. I mean, my face was in a fight, as were my ribs, but I most assuredly was not." I unbuttoned my shirt and slid it off, marveling at the enormous shoe-shaped bruise on my side. If my guess was right, Ben wore a size nine. "And before you ask, my face lost."

Quinn's brow was furrowed. He kept shaking his head, as if his denial of my predicament would somehow help the situation. "Is there anything I can do?"

"Hand me the medical kit from the cabinet in the hall? And maybe grab me some ice?" He left the room immediately, and I caught my reflection in our television screen. I looked much worse than I felt, which was saying something. Maybe the adrenaline was kicking in. About ten minutes too late, but I'd take what I could get.

The last fight I had been in was in the third grade. I'd been examining a colony of ants with a magnifying glass and a boy who lived nearby had insisted on killing them instead. I'd shoved him, starting the fight. He'd creamed me, finishing it. I hadn't been in a fight ever since. It just wasn't my strength, or my style.

When Quinn returned to the room, he handed me the medical kit and started gathering ice from the tray in our small freezer, wrapping it inside a towel for my face. "Who was it?"

"Three total assholes with very large fists—one by the name of Ben Winchester." Inside the kit were several small antibacterial wipes. They stung as I dabbed at the open wounds on my face. Quinn sat down on the bed beside me, looking more than a little concerned. "Ben used to come over and play in my sandbox with me when I was in kindergarten. Suffice it to say, I won't be inviting him over again anytime soon."

"Maybe you should go to the nurse. I think she's on call twenty-four-seven."

"And say what? That I was at an unauthorized party and got the crap beat out of me?" Tossing the wipes into the trash, I stood up and made my way to the bathroom. Every time I inhaled, my side lit up with pain. "That's just not how I roll, Quinn. Besides, there's nothing she can do that I can't. Clean it up, take a few Tylenol, slap a butterfly bandage on the cut over my eye, and voilà. It's like I've been to nursing school."

Quinn's shoulders sank in apparent insult. "My mom's a nurse."

He handed me the towel filled with ice, and I felt like such a tool. "I'm sorry. I'm just . . . trying to figure out how to get my life back."

"You could start by not being so much of a jerk." The hurt was evident in his eyes. You could do a lot to a guy, say a lot about him. But don't mess with his mom. That was an uncrossable line.

"You're all right, Quinn." I pressed the cool towel to my eye and the bridge of my nose. "And what's more, you're right."

He nodded, accepting my unspoken apology, even though he didn't have to. "Your nose is bleeding."

Sure enough, drops of crimson dripped from my nose to the white porcelain of the sink below. Quinn stepped out of the room, leaving me to fix myself up. I stared at my reflection in the mirror for a while, wondering what Viktor would say about this when I saw him the next night. Turning on the water, I washed my face carefully, making sure my skin was dry before I applied a bandage to the cut above my eye.

The attack had seemed so random, so strange. Again, I wondered if it had been some kind of setup. But why? To get me to want to go back to California sooner? If so, mission accomplished.

Inside my pocket, my phone buzzed. When I withdrew it, I saw a text from my anonymous source. After a few days of silence, I'd let myself hope that the messages might have stopped for good.

Grace and her boy toy are celebrating right now. Are you seriously going to just take it?

No. No, I wasn't, my anonymous friend.

I shoved a wad of toilet paper in my bleeding nostril and left the room in a hurry. I was on the warpath, and I knew exactly where I was headed. My rising adrenaline was doing its best to keep my pain under control as I moved.

On my way, I passed Caroline on the sidewalk outside the library. She looked horrified at my current condition. "What happened to you?"

I didn't even slow my steps. My words came out in a growl. "Tea party in the garden with the queen. She plays a mean game of chess."

She called after me, "Are you okay?"

"I'm fine. It's no big deal. Really." I said it more to myself than to her. But it was a lie, and I knew it.

"I guess I'm glad I didn't go to the party, huh?"

"Very funny." She looked genuinely sorry for me, and maybe something else, too.

"Hey, Adrien? I was thinking we could work on our experiment on Sunday so we're ready for next week. If we go to the soccer field first thing, Coach Taryn will be there with the lacrosse team, so we'd have our staff supervision."

"Sure, Sunday at nine. Anything else?"

She could tell I was a guy on a mission.

"Nope. See you then."

Moments later, I pulled open the door to the radio station without knocking.

Grace and Josh were on the couch, lips locked. A celebratory kiss, maybe? I didn't care. I grabbed Josh by the collar and pulled back my fist. When I let it loose and slammed it into his nose, my hand felt like it had snapped. Maybe I'd broken it. I had no idea. I'd never really hit anyone with a closed fist before, and I was too far beyond anger to feel much pain. Thank you, adrenaline.

Blood burst from Josh's nose and he made a gurgling sound. Some of his blood spattered onto the front of Grace's shirt. Pulling him closer by the collar, I growled into his dazed expression, "That's for setting me up. And this is for screwing my sister."

I punched him again and Josh fell to the floor in a heap.

The walk back to my room was a heated blur.

[CHAPTER 10]

IMMISCIBLE:

When two liquids do not form
a solution with each other

It was early the next morning when Josh opened my door
without knocking, but not so early that I wasn't already up
and dressed in a black tee and jeans. I sat at my desk, waiting, looking at Twitter on my phone, making note of the
fact that Grace had been chatting with my attackers just the
morning before, asking if they were excited about the party.
Of course. Of course she had.

I knew Josh would be coming for me. Probably to kick
my ass. I'd barely slept, my eyes on the door throughout
the night, wondering when his retaliation would begin. I'd
left the door unlocked because I wanted to prove to myself

that I wasn't a coward. I'd felt cowardly enough lying on the ground last night, wishing my mother could magically appear and comfort me.

Beneath Josh's eyes were purple half-moons. His nose was swollen slightly. I couldn't tell if it was broken or not. My hand still hurt like hell.

He sat down on my bed, not saying anything for a long time. When he finally spoke, he sounded more exasperated than angry. His voice was hushed. "Why'd you hit me?"

I didn't look up from my phone. As I gripped it tighter, my knuckles throbbed. I'd never hit anyone before, so it hadn't really occurred to me that it might hurt my hand. As nonchalantly as I could manage, I said, "Because you set me up to get my ass beat by three Neanderthals just to get on Grace's good side. And you screwed my sister."

"I didn't set you up."

I sat the pen down and met Josh's eyes. "But you did screw my sister."

He ran a hand through his hair, brushing it back from his face, and as he did, I saw how swollen the bridge of his nose really was. As much as I wasn't a fan of violence, I was pretty proud that I'd managed to do some noticeable damage my first time out. But on the heels of that pride came immense guilt. This was Josh. He'd been my best friend once. How could I have done that to him?

He took a deep breath and blew it out, meeting my eyes. "What exactly happened last night after I left the party?"

"What happened?" I raised my voice, infuriated that he would dare play dumb over something he'd obviously had a hand in. "Some girl lured me outside and then your friends took quite a pounding on me. I'm sure that made for some fantastic foreplay for you and Grace. Lead me to some party where a girl gets me alone and three guys beat the crap out of me. For what? Why, Josh? Why?"

Josh shook his head, his expression troubled. "I don't know what you're talking about. I left a note on Grace's door asking her if we could talk at the party. She showed up, we went for a walk, and ended up in the station. She kissed me, then you came in and punched me twice, and then she went back to her room. Help me out here, Adrien. Because I'm lost."

"I can't trust you, Josh. I can't trust anyone around here!" I stood, throwing my hands in the air. "How could you sleep with her, knowing what she had just done to me?"

He shook his head, standing. We were less than a foot apart. "Listen. You are being so paranoid, I'm not even sure you can, but please try to listen. You have no reason to believe me, but I had nothing to do with whatever went down at the party last night. And despite what it may have looked like, I've never slept with your sister."

I jabbed my finger into his chest. "Bullshit."

"I wanted to tell her something last night—something I thought might make her feel better about our breakup. But after I told her, she kissed me. Maybe she thought she could change my mind, I don't know." His tone wasn't accusatory at all. He was just laying out what had happened. Or what he wanted me to believe had happened.

"Then why would she say before that you screwed her?"

"I don't know. Maybe because she was mad at me for breaking up with her. Maybe she knew it would bother you to think I had. Or maybe she was just embarrassed because I wouldn't sleep with her."

That was rich. "Right. You said you two went out all last year."

"We did."

"But you never slept together? Not once? In a year?"

"No."

"You're such a liar, Josh."

"No, I'm not, goddammit!" His chest was rising and falling in hurried breaths. For a moment, I knew that he was going to hit me. And it was going to hurt. "I'm not lying. I'm trying to tell you something, you ass. And this isn't at all how I wanted to tell you."

"Tell me? Tell me what?" I readied my stance, spreading my feet slowly apart so I could keep my balance when the time for a fight came.

Josh shook his head, his cheeks flushed. "I don't think I can, Adrien. You might never speak to me again."

I balled my hands into fists, staring him down. "Well I definitely won't speak to you again if you don't just find the balls to tell me whatever you're holding back from me!"

"Fine!" His green eyes gleamed with something that I didn't yet understand. He reached up with his right hand, raking his fingers through my hair. Before I realized what was happening, Josh pulled me close to him, pressing his warm mouth to mine. He parted his lips, and, without thinking, as if it were the most natural reaction in the world, I slid my tongue into his mouth. For a moment that stretched on forever, we kissed, deeply, our hearts pounding together through cotton. The scruff on his chin scraped gently against mine, sending a shiver of longing down my spine. His hands slid from my hair to either side of my face, his teeth gently biting my bottom lip for a moment. He held me there, and I moved my hands to his hips, pulling him closer. I couldn't think, didn't want to think. I just wanted this feeling to go on forever. A small moan escaped him and his hands lifted my T-shirt up some, so that his palms were against my skin. I slowly slid my hands up his sides, over his shoulders, down his arms. My hands were on his wrists when at last we parted, ever so slowly.

I felt as if all the air had been sucked from my lungs. My

heart was racing. I didn't know what to say. He didn't speak, just looked into my eyes with a sad questioning. When I could breathe again, my trembling fingertips left his wrists and found my lips. I knew I had to say something, but words escaped me. Finally, with a shaking breath, I whispered, "Oh . . ."

Josh was still standing very close to me, his chest rising and falling just as quickly as mine. I wasn't certain whether I wanted him to move away or come even closer. My head was in a fog. His eyes were locked on mine, but though there was sadness there, I saw no apology. All he said was, "Yeah . . ."

After a moment—a strange moment full of longing and fear—Josh took the initiative and stepped back. But even his distance failed to cool the air between us. His eyes shimmered slightly. "You hate me now? You must. I shouldn't have—"

"No." The word leapt from my mouth before I could even think it, but that didn't change the fact that I meant it. I could still taste his kiss on my lips, the scrape of his stubble on my chin as I reached for my hoodie and moved to the door. When I looked back at him, I didn't know how to respond exactly to what had just transpired. I just knew that my heart was still racing, and that a large part of me didn't want to walk out of that room. I didn't even know where I was going, only that I couldn't stay. With great reluctance, I pulled the door open, and as I turned back to him, I said, "No, Josh. I don't hate you. I could never hate you. I just . . . I've gotta go."

He swallowed hard. "Yeah . . . me too."

Stepping into the hall was like waking from a dream. I had kissed boys before, but not like that, not in a way that made me want to go on kissing him forever. Or even progressing past that point of just lips on lips and tongues intertwined. If I'd stayed, I might have . . . we might have— no. We *would have* done more. I know we would have.

As I hurried down the hall, I wrestled with why I'd walked out. Clearly, that intimacy had been a moment we'd both wanted to share. So what was I afraid of?

I didn't know. I didn't know what I was afraid of, or if I was afraid of anything at all. I just knew that Josh was my best friend here (and a great kisser), that he was one of the only people even on my side at Wills (and had such broad shoulders), and that if I lost him, I didn't know what I would do.

So I wandered the building for several minutes, catching my breath, trying not to think about how that kiss had felt, how it reverberated through my body still. I wasn't sure where to go or what to do. I certainly didn't want to talk to anybody about it. To be honest, I wanted to go somewhere where I could be alone and just relish the moment without fear of what that moment might have changed, or what it might mean in the big scheme of things. I wanted to get away from here. But to where? And how?

After a while, I stopped by my mailbox at the front desk. To my surprise, an envelope was waiting there from Viktor. Inside were a second set of car keys and a note that read, *I trust you'll repay me for the tune-up and new tires. Enjoy. —V*

As I stepped outside, the cool air hit me like that first blast of air conditioning on a hot day. I looked across the parking lot and there she was. Maggie. Just when I needed her most. Viktor had an uncanny ability to provide me with precisely what I needed when I needed it, even when he had no idea that he was doing so.

I moved to her and unlocked the door, silently thanking Viktor with all my soul. I slid into the driver's seat and rested my aching head on the steering wheel for several minutes. Then I whispered, "Now what, Maggie? Now what?"

I wasn't just asking her where we should go, what we should do. I was asking her so much more than that—things I suspected only she would understand.

Sliding the key into the ignition, I turned it and gave her some gas. Maggie's engine roared to life. She was loud and angry and the only one on my side. As I put her in drive, I said, "You're right. Let's get the hell outta here."

I slammed my foot on the gas pedal, and Maggie's tires spun with fury, leaving a cloud of smoke behind us as we peeled out of the school parking lot. We didn't know where we were going or when we would come back. We just knew that we needed to be alone. Together.

We drove for hours, sticking mostly to the back roads where Maggie could really open up and fly without worrying about cops. I stopped for gas when I had to, and avoided gravel when I could. But some of the dirt roads had curves that Maggie begged to whip around, and I could refuse her nothing. She was a badass beauty, a kickass tough girl who would take no shit and take no prisoners. And before I knew it, the sun was setting.

There was no time to head back to the dorms to clean up and change. And I wasn't exactly in the mood to give a shit about how I looked for some stupid dinner party. Besides, it was probably better that I wasn't going back to campus—I still needed time to think about what I was supposed to say to Josh when I saw him again.

As I pulled up to Viktor's estate, I cursed under my breath. Several upscale cars had been parked neatly off to the side by one of two valets. The people I saw walking inside were dressed impeccably, the men in suits and even a few tuxes. Viktor was going to be pissed that I'd come in jeans and a T-shirt. Not to mention the bruises and swelling on my face.

I pulled Maggie up on the right, well away from the other

partygoers' vehicles. As I stepped out and shut the door, one of the valet guys shouted to me, "Hey, buddy, you can't park that here."

"It's okay, Andrew." Julian stepped out onto the walkway. As usual, he was dressed in a suit, his shirt perfectly ironed, his blue tie straight as an arrow. He looked at the valet and forced a smile. "This is Mr. Dane. He's on the guest list."

The valet nodded to me, looking somewhat embarrassed and a little more than confused. "My apologies, sir."

I hated when people called me sir, but I just shrugged as I stepped onto the walkway that led to the front stairs. "No big deal."

Julian placed a well-manicured hand on my shoulder and looked me over, from my sneakers to my jeans, up to my T-shirt, and, at last, to my damaged face. He sighed with a thick air of disapproval. "What are we going to do with you, Adrien?"

"Hey, if tonight doesn't end with me getting a black eye, I'm calling it a success." I smirked, but Julian's stony exterior didn't even crack. He was pissed. I could see that much in his eyes alone—never mind the way his jaw seemed to tighten at my attempt at humor.

I started to walk around him, but he stopped me. His tone indicated he meant business. "Go in the back door and change upstairs into something more suitable. If anyone asks about your bruises, you were in a car accident, but nothing serious. I don't want you ruining something that Viktor worked very hard to set up."

"Now, now, Julian. You know how Viktor feels about lying." I looked up at the house, surprised by the formality of the evening. All I'd been told was to wear a tie. How was I supposed to know? "Quite the party. I was under the impression it was just a dinner."

"Not just any dinner. He's invited a lot of important people who most Wills students would kill to rub elbows with. He's doing you an enormous favor, and you thank him by showing up looking like a homeless rat who's just been in a bar fight." He stepped to the side, pointing to the house with the rocks glass he was holding. The ice inside rattled a bit. "Now. Back door. As quickly and quietly as you can. There are clothes in your room. And for god's sake, use an iron."

There was something appealing about the idea of seeing just how far I could push Julian. But as tempted as I was to stroll in the front door dressed like I was, I knew that the sight of me would disappoint Viktor, and that I didn't want. So I walked around the side of the house and opened the back door. I slid inside and moved through the kitchen soundlessly, then up the back stairs. After washing my face in the small bathroom connected to my room, I opened the closet door and sighed. I didn't want to be here. Not in this room. Not at this party. Not in this moment. But what else could I do?

Once I'd changed into a pair of black slacks and a red button-up shirt that didn't seem *too* wrinkled, I threw on a black tie and belt and headed downstairs, hoping that Viktor would be too distracted by his many guests to take real notice of the bruises on my face.

Running a hand through the mop of hair on my head, I made my way down the front stairwell. The first voice I heard belonged to Viktor, who was standing at the bottom of the steps with none other than Grace. She wore a simple black knee-length dress and heels. He was dressed in a gray three-piece suit, holding a glass of white wine. "Adrien. I'm so glad you could make it."

My steps slowed as I descended, but I kept going until I was standing in front of him. I didn't know why I was ashamed of the bruises. Maybe because I wasn't that kind of guy. Maybe because I still didn't understand the reasons behind my face getting creamed. Maybe because I'd lost, and I didn't want Viktor to see me as a loser.

I forced a smile but knew it wasn't very convincing. "Wouldn't miss it for the world."

"Better a late arrival than no arrival at all." He put his arm around my shoulder and cast a sympathetic look at my wounded face. Then he held out his other arm for Grace and led us toward the den. "Come. I want to speak to you two in private for a moment."

As we moved down the hall, one of the servers held out a silver tray of glasses. I said, "What are they?"

"This side is nonalcoholic cranberry spritzers. This side's got cosmopolitans. But you're a little young for those." He smiled and I smiled back.

"Indeed, I am," I said as I took a spritzer in my hand. But the moment Viktor turned his back, I switched it out for a cosmo. Maybe I didn't drink. But I didn't fight, either.

As Viktor, Grace, and I stepped into the den, Julian gave my shirt a disapproving once-over and whispered to me, "Play nice."

What was that supposed to mean? Grace was the one who started shit. All I ever wanted was to finish it.

Once the doors were closed, Viktor smiled warmly at us both. "It's good to see you both, children."

"Likewise, Uncle." Grace sat on the chaise and folded her hands neatly in her lap. Her hair was curled into ringlets that lay over her right shoulder.

"And it's nice to see you two getting along. Even if it is merely a lie perpetuated by Julian." I shot a glance to Grace, who was already looking at me in wonder. Apparently we weren't the great actors we thought we were. "Come, now. Do you really think I'm that stupid?"

Grace began to say, "We never—"

"It's quite all right. If I can't get you two to come together as a family, at least I can pretend for a short while that you won't strangle each other in my parlor." Viktor moved to his desk and opened the top drawer. From it, he removed a manila envelope that looked stuffed to the gills. "Now, as to why I wanted to speak with you . . ."

I didn't speak, couldn't speak. I couldn't even move. The whole room felt like it was filling with a thick, hot gas. I knew this sensation. We were about to talk about death. Viktor's death.

He said, "I didn't want you to find this out after I've passed on. Julian knows, and he supports my decision. But I've decided that I want to tell you in person why I'm not leaving any of my estate to either of you." Grace sat up some in her seat. I didn't move. "Instead I'm leaving the entirety to the Wills Institute. All but a modest stipend for Julian." It was unexpected, but it was also just money.

I counted two heartbeats before I let the words leave my mouth—words I already knew the answer to. "Does he . . . know that you're dying, then?"

Grace's eyes snapped to me in a warning—Julian had probably talked to her about it, too—but I simply shrugged in response. We were all dancing around the issue, and I was quickly tiring of it. The last semblance of family that we had would soon be leaving us forever. I didn't get why we were pretending that he was going to be alive in another year or two or ten. The sky was blue. Water was wet. And Viktor was dying. It was just the way of things.

"Yes. I suspect he's known for some time, but this past week, I told him myself." For a moment, a profound sadness filled his eyes. Then, as if gathering himself once again, he took on a businesslike tone. "Do you understand the importance of my decision to will my estate to Wills?"

Grace and I spoke at the same time—probably the only time we had ever agreed on anything, even if it was only a choice of words. "Of course."

"I just didn't want either of you to feel left out. I care deeply for both of you. But I think the money would do better to serve many children, rather than just two, and of course you have the trust from your parents."

"Don't worry about it, Viktor. I'm not." I downed the last of my cosmo and set the glass on the desk.

As I stood, Viktor's eyes shimmered. He said, "I cannot possibly express to you how much I will miss you both."

Grace stood and rushed across the room, hugging him tightly. "Oh, Uncle . . ."

"The time for good-byes is fast approaching, children. I want nothing unsaid when it comes." As he embraced my sister, he looked at me, his eyes now filled with visible tears.

"I love you. Both of you. I never had children of my own, but I always viewed you both as such. After I am gone, only the two of you and my beloved Julian will remain. Take care of one another. Please. All of you."

It was too much—the idea of losing Viktor. I'd known for over eight days now, but it hadn't seemed real until this very moment. Viktor was dying. And soon all I'd have left to call family would be Grace. It wasn't right. It wasn't fair.

I walked out of the room and snagged another cosmo, then found a quiet corner of the house to hide in until it was announced that dinner was being served. I counted roughly twenty people gathering around the table—by the looks of it, power players, maybe a few academics, and me. An older gentleman to my left swallowed a bite of something creamy and green before meeting my eyes. "I knew your father well, Mr. Dane. Tell me. Do you plan to follow in his career footsteps? He was a brilliant chemist, and a marvelous teacher."

My face was feeling warm. It was a pleasant warmth, and one that made it easier to make small talk. I blamed the booze. With a shrug, I said, "I might follow him into chemistry, but not teaching. To be honest, I haven't given it that much thought just yet."

The man dabbed at the corners of his mouth with his cloth napkin, then returned the napkin to his lap. He looked somewhat perplexed by my response. "It is your senior year, isn't it?"

The rest of the table had turned their attention to our conversation. I took a sip of water and set it down, gathering my thoughts. "Yes. It is my senior year. But anyone who thinks that an eighteen-year-old is capable of choosing their forever path in life is kidding themselves. I'll figure it out. I just need time. And patience."

"Adrien has a brilliant mind. He just needs the right people behind him to encourage him and show him how to apply himself. I expect wonderful things from him, given time." From the opposite end of the table, Viktor raised his glass to me in a toasting gesture and smiled. "And patience."

A woman in peach chiffon addressed my sister then. "What about you, Grace? Do you find yourself requiring more time to find your chosen path in life?"

Grace, as usual, had all the right answers. "I plan to work in pharmaceuticals. In fact, I'm confidently planning to apply to all the Ivy Leagues when the time comes."

"Of course you are," I muttered under my breath, earning a look of warning from Julian.

Looking down the table to my godfather, I silently thought to him, *Why am I here?*

But Viktor and I had been having conversations with

our eyes for years, and the way he was looking at me now, I imagined his response was something like, *Because sometimes a brief, pleasant dinner conversation can open a door years later that you weren't even aware existed. Now, if I could trouble you to be your charming self for the remainder of the evening?*

His smile came slowly but surely—the way it always did when he was certain he knew what he was talking about. When it appeared, I found myself letting go of my urge to leave the table. Viktor had always had that effect on me. He was soothing, calming. When he smiled at me, it felt like being wrapped up in a blanket after coming in from the cold.

I was going to miss him.

I spent the rest of the dinner nibbling on small bites and engaging in small talk to make him happy. I even promised a man who owned a few biomedical companies around the country that I would look him up after I finished school (whenever I finished school).

It helped to pretend that Grace wasn't sitting across from me, judging me with her effortless ability to talk to strangers. It helped more that I'd managed to sneak another cosmo when nobody was paying attention. After dessert and coffee, Viktor and Julian gave their good-byes and escorted guests to the door. Grace and I were the only two left at the table, but neither of us spoke. My phone buzzed in my pocket, and when I retrieved it, I saw that my mysterious informant had just texted me. They said, **Grace has evidence of what really happened to your parents. Find it!**

I glanced toward the door long enough to see something that made my heart skip a beat. Julian was texting someone. Another message popped up on my phone. **Might I suggest you check her room?**

I sat there dumbfounded. Could Julian be the person who'd been tormenting me with these text messages? Why?

Grace raised a well-manicured brow in my general direction. "Are you staying here tonight or going back to the dorms?"

The room tilted slightly, so I said, "Staying."

"Good. I'd hate for you to die in some horrible car accident after sneaking so much to drink." She smiled in that sweet, sadistic way of hers before walking around the table to leave the room.

As she passed behind my chair, I emptied my glass and said, "You'd like that, wouldn't you?"

She paused, but only briefly.

"Oh, brother . . ." She bent down, whispering in my ear. I could feel her breath brush the tiny hairs on my neck, my skin turning to gooseflesh, as if reacting to the poison of her words. "I'd revel in it."

I had no idea why some people were vile and others were not. Maybe they really were that way when they were born.

After all, we'd had the same parents—it was hard to say Grace was a product of bad nurturing. Still, maybe experience made them that way. We might have lived inside the same house, but Grace and I had led very different lives. It was hard to think of a control group to even test a hypothesis. I'd met people like Grace of all genders, races, and orientations. Nothing seemed to tie them together but the bitterness that fueled their words . . . and my exhaustion over having met them.

"You're a kind person, Grace." I raised my empty glass in her direction. The room was feeling warmer than I remembered, and a lot less stable. Were the walls really spinning or was it just my perception? "Mom and Dad would be proud."

I wasn't sure where he'd come from or when, but Julian was standing over me, his jaw set, his eyes full of disapproval. I set my glass on the table and said, "It's just a cranberry spritzer."

"Please. Lying is so unbecoming of you." He took my glass, despite the fact that it was empty. Then he bent closer to my ear and hissed, "Seems like you've had enough. More than enough, considering you're only eighteen. What were you thinking? That no one would notice?"

That wasn't it at all. I wasn't even sure what it was, why I'd drunk, especially so much. I'd thought I could come back here, to the place where I'd grown up, and not completely lose myself. I was wrong.

I stood. I wanted my actions to be strong and smooth, but I staggered a little as I pushed my chair back from the table. "Julian, you're not my father."

I looked him in the eye, hardly caring in that moment whether it *had* been Julian texting me about Grace and the evidence she supposedly had about the fire that killed our parents. As I moved past him and up the stairs, I said, "He's dead."

[CHAPTER 11]

NUCLEAR REACTION:
Any process in which the nucleus of an atom is changed in some fashion

That night I didn't sleep so much as move in and out of consciousness on a wave of nausea. Once I'd sobered up, I drove Maggie back to the dorms in the wee hours of morning and took a hot shower. My head felt like it was floating somewhere above my body, and my everything hurt. It had been stupid to drink. Alcohol was a poison, and consuming it would serve to get a person nowhere fast. It wasn't logical to poison yourself, and it had been proven in my case to lead to negative outcomes. But then . . . I hadn't been feeling very logical lately.

Caroline was waiting for me beside the soccer field at

9:00 a.m., as promised. We went over our notes in silence, recording our method and double-checking that we had the right amounts of potassium and water. Finally, she handed me a pair of goggles and said, "You look like hell. Did your weekend get worse after the last time I saw you?"

I took off my sunglasses, squinting at the light of the sun, and hung them from my left jeans pocket. "Dinner party on Saturday, hangover on Sunday."

She frowned, her pink lips sinking in concern. "I'm worried about you."

"Don't worry about me. Worry about this garbage can. Are we all set?" I glanced over at Coach Taryn, who had put the lacrosse team to work running laps and now eyed us warily. I wasn't worried about the garbage can blowing up so dramatically that it might hurt the players all the way over there, but I didn't want a screaming coach on my back this early in the morning.

"Thirty grams of potassium. Sealed trash can. Goggles on. Let's do this." She signaled our supervisor with a nod and shouted, "Coach Taryn?"

He gave us a thumbs-up.

Caroline clutched the string that was dangling the potassium over the water inside the trash can. I opened the scissors and placed them around the string. "One . . . two . . . three!"

I cut the string, and we both held our breath as the potassium dropped into the water. For a moment nothing happened. Then an explosion of steam blew the lid off the trash can. The chemical reaction reached up into the sky, forming a mini mushroom cloud of sorts. Impressive on a visual level. The trash can, however, stood unharmed. I sighed. Caroline groaned. "That sucked! It didn't even dent the can. It just blew the lid off. How are we going to blow up a bathtub?"

Our calculations were off. Way off. It should have been far more fantastic than it actually was. I was off my game, clearly. "We need more potassium. A lot more potassium."

Caroline rolled her eyes at my obvious assessment of the situation. "Ya think?"

"Well, recalculations are part of the process. Every failure is a success that we learn from." I didn't even feel like I was there, in that field, going through the motions of a scientific experiment. My mind felt like it was somewhere else entirely, though I couldn't pinpoint where exactly. Maybe California.

Caroline met my gaze. "What did you learn from your hangover?"

"That vodka is something to be avoided in the future." My stomach flip-flopped in response. It didn't want to talk about vodka. It just wanted to go back to my room and lie down for a while. "Can I ask you something?"

"Of course."

"Do you want to go out sometime? Like for a ride or something? Maybe pizza?"

She picked up the now-dented lid of our trash can. "Absolutely. But no one ever asks me."

I paused, taking a moment to figure out whether or not she was joking. The look in her eyes said that she really had no idea that I'd done just that. "I'm asking you."

"Oh." At first she looked surprised. Then she shook her head. "No. Sorry."

As she walked toward our failed experiment, I followed, shaking my head. Was I really that bad? I thought of the look in her eye on Friday night, when she'd invited me to meet her this morning. It hadn't seemed like it was just for the science experiment. "What is it with you? You don't like me or something?"

She shrugged. "I told you. I'm just not interested in you in that way."

"It's not a date. It's just a ride with a friend. And *maybe* pizza." I put on my most charming smile. At least, as charming as I could be when I felt like my head was full of sharp shards of rock. "If you're lucky."

But I wasn't just asking her out as a friend, and I knew it. A little voice at the back of my mind questioned whether me asking Caroline out had anything at all to do with Josh kissing me the day before. I swore to myself that the two had nothing to do with each other, but honestly? What I did know was how it had felt to kiss Josh. What I didn't know was what it might feel like to kiss Caroline.

She looked me over for a moment, as if debating just how terrible an evening with me might be. It didn't exactly inspire confidence in my fragile ego. Finally, she hoisted up the trash can and said, "Okay. But we're just friends."

"Fine." There was something way too formal about the whole thing. I'd hung out with friends plenty of times before. Why was she making this awkward? Or was that just her deal? Maybe she was just an awkward person. The evidence was certainly pointing in that direction. "Tonight? Say eight o'clock?"

"Fine."

We cleaned up our experiment and yelled our thanks to Coach Taryn for his supervision. Afterward, I headed back to my room, where my pillow was calling my name. I was certain from what little experience I had that sleep was the only thing that was going to ease my throbbing head.

As I moved into the dorm, silence enveloped me. This evening would be different. Commuter students would return from their weekends at home, and with them would come the hustle and bustle and noise of dormitory living.

But for now, it was still early, and the halls were blissfully silent. I was looking forward to a nice nap.

I trudged up the main stairs of the dormitory, anxious to reach my room. My footfalls echoed as I climbed toward the top floor. I did my best to tread lightly. Not because I was afraid of disturbing anyone, but because I wanted to see if I could step softly enough that the sound wouldn't reverberate off the stone walls around me. I was in a battle with the laws of physics. It was stupid, but people do a lot of stupid things when no one is looking.

I finally reached the top floor and hung a left toward the tower stairs. The tile floor of the hall coupled with the addition of wooden doors caused me to change my strategy slightly. Then a loud slam from the end of the hall thundered through my aching head, causing me to lose this particular battle.

The echo of voices had replaced the echo of my steps. The sound grew louder as the speakers came closer. There were two voices. Both rang at a higher timbre, definitely female. What's more, I recognized one of them as Penelope's, and the other voice belonged to Grace.

"I got it. I should have had it four years ago, but I've got it now." Grace's words piqued my interest. What was it that she had? But I was in no mood to ask her. The way I was feeling at the moment, I thought it best if she didn't even see me. The last thing I wanted right now was to get into another argument with her. I ducked back into the doorway of the janitor's closet, staying out of sight as they made their way to the stairs.

"I'm so excited for you. I'm already sick of seeing Adrien's face and he's only been here a week." I could hear them as they started to descend the stairs.

Their voices were fading as they rounded the landing one floor beneath me. "Listen, I have to go pick something up. I'll meet you in the dining hall in fifteen minutes, okay?"

So much for my nap. Headache or no headache, this was my chance to find out exactly where Grace had been going and what she'd been up to. And this time, I knew where Penelope would be, so there was no chance that she could get in my way.

I made my way down the stairs and out into the morning air just in time to see Grace and Penelope part ways. I tried to act casual as I walked across the campus grounds, but I had to be quick or I would lose her.

It didn't take long for me to figure out where she was headed. I'd seen Grace take this path a hundred times. She was headed for the library. Of course, as I'd learned on Friday night, it probably wasn't the books she'd been visiting at all. It was probably the radio station on the third floor.

But then it occurred to me I'd caught her slipping out the back door of the library before. Once, I'd even seen her do so when I'd been visiting Josh myself, so there was no way she'd been in the radio station.

Deciding to test the hypothesis that was taking shape in my mind, I waited for her to head into the library, then rounded the building to the back and hid in the shadows behind the recycling bin. Sure enough, before long the back door to the library opened, spilling light out into the nearly enclosed parking lot. Grace exited the building and turned toward me. Her stride was confident and direct, as if she'd walked this route so often it was a routine. I ducked down, peering between the Dumpster and the wall. Grace stood at a locked door I'd assumed led to a maintenance room. She paused and looked around before retrieving a key from her pocket. Opening the padlock, Grace yanked on the door and went inside.

I moved around the Dumpster toward the door. Whatever she was doing in there, I knew that it couldn't be good for me. I had to find out what it was. I reached for the door handle. If I could just get it open a crack, I might be able to get some idea of what she was up to.

As my hand began to close around the handle, I felt it turn from the inside. Grace was coming out. A crack of yellow light spilled outside, and I had microseconds before I was caught. In a moment of panic, I reached out with my leg and kicked the door as hard as I could. It slammed closed. I picked up a glass bottle from beside the recycling bin and ran for the front of the library. The door started to open again. I threw the bottle behind me, and it shattered into pieces when it struck the block building. I could hear Grace yelling from inside the mystery room.

"Real mature, jerk!" She hadn't seen me. Well, she had seen someone, but I didn't think she knew it was me.

I didn't stop running until I got back to my room. I grabbed my messenger bag and some supplies, then headed right back out. My earlier headache was gone. I couldn't even think about sleeping anymore. It had taken me this long to find out where Grace had been going all this time. I wasn't about to waste any more time wondering what she was doing.

The only variable in my plan was where my sister was now. It would put a serious damper on my investigation if she were to walk in on me going through her secret lair. But as much as I liked to eliminate variables, that was a risk I was willing to take.

I made my way out of the dorm and back to the library. I took a couple of paper clips out of my bag. I bent the end of one and inserted it into the padlock. After ten minutes of twisting and swearing, I remembered that I had no idea how to pick a lock. I'd seen it done on TV and read about it in several novels, but it turned out that TV and novels were not necessarily accurate representations of real life. I decided to take a much more scientific approach. If I couldn't pick the lock, I'd just break the damn thing instead.

Reaching back into my trusty bag of tricks, I grabbed my can of compressed air. It was a simple-enough tool. I'd purchased this particular can right here at the campus bookstore. Sure, it was great for cleaning the dust and debris from one's computer and keyboard, but who knew that it was so helpful when breaking and entering?

I slid the red straw into the padlock that I had seen my sister open less than a half hour earlier and pressed the button. The trapped carbon dioxide gas inside hissed as it escaped its cylindrical prison. The lock grew white with frost as it chilled from the inside out. I picked up a large rock and slammed it against the lock. It shattered like glass, and I opened the door. Videos on YouTube had shown me several examples of it working, but I stood there in shock for a moment. I wasn't actually sure how much the canned air helped, but the rock definitely did wonders.

I flipped the light switch and waited for my eyes to adjust to the low yellow light. What lay before me sent a chill up my spine while simultaneously sending flames up the side of my face. I was in a lab. A chemistry lab. Grace's lab.

There were glass bottles full of chemicals lining metal

shelves on the walls. Various acids and solutions were neatly labeled and placed so that those in danger of reacting were as far away from one another as possible. There were jars of raw elements as well. Sodium, potassium, cesium. Several of them could be quite volatile if not properly handled. Beakers and test tubes lined a drying rack near the sink. A Bunsen burner was attached to a large green cylinder with a hose.

I made my way down the three steps and onto the floor of my sister's laboratory. Her experimental notes were sitting out on the table. I picked up the top sheet of paper and my heart sank. I instantly recognized what she was doing. These were my father's formulas, in my father's handwriting. This was my father's life's work. The formulas he'd been developing to create temporary night vision for a variety of purposes with nothing more than some brilliantly concocted eye drops.

On the table next to his notes was an experiment log book that she'd obviously been working on for some time. It looked almost ready to be turned into a paper for presentation. I leaned back against the table. The mysterious texter had been right all along. Grace was going to take credit for my father's work.

I started gathering Grace's and our parents' notes together. I was taking them. I was taking it all. I'd be damned if she was going to take credit for Dad's biggest dream and all of his and our mom's hard work. I picked up the last notebook from the table and added it to my pile, swearing under my breath as I did. This was my father's notebook. The one I had picked up from the burnt remains of our home the day our parents died. This must have been what Grace and Penelope had been grabbing from my room earlier.

I set down the stack and flipped open the notebook. Loose pages came fluttering out, falling to the floor at my feet. I picked them up and started to read the words written on them. I didn't recognize these words. I had read my father's journal—at least what I had of it—countless times over the last four years, but I didn't recognize these pages. I turned to the section that had been ripped out—and held one of the loose pages up to the tear. These were the missing pages from my father's journal, reunited with their home at last.

What did she hope to accomplish from stealing his work, exactly? Was this about getting into an Ivy League school? I was the one who'd assisted Dad in the lab. Did she hope to erase my involvement completely? Or was this about the money she could get from selling the work, plain and simple? I remembered what she had said at the dinner party the night before about going into pharmaceuticals. How like Grace to turn this all into a horrible joke.

CHAPTER 12

SECOND LAW OF THERMODYNAMICS:

The randomness of the universe is always increasing

"Ya know what?" I chewed the bite of cheese, dough, and pepperoni in my mouth and swallowed, chasing it down with a swig of cola. Maggie's hood was still warm beneath me, even though we'd been out here for almost an hour.

It was well after curfew, but that just meant the drop-off overlooking the campus was empty and quiet. The sky stretched on forever above us, framed by the shadowy treetops. It might have been a perfect evening . . . if I had any idea what I was doing out here with Caroline. We weren't on a date. I wasn't even sure I thought about her in that way. Not that I could think about much of anything but Grace's secret lab. No matter what I did, my mind just kept trailing back to Grace. Caroline deserved better than that.

"What?" Caroline was wearing a worn-out band T-shirt and ripped jeans under an oversized camouflage jacket that looked like she'd picked it up at the military surplus store or something. There was a rank insignia on the sleeve. I thought it might have been for a staff sergeant, but couldn't be sure—I hadn't played enough Call of Duty to recognize rank, apparently. Maybe it had belonged to her dad or something. I didn't ask. I kept wondering if she was cold but didn't say anything about it. It was weird to see her in anything that wasn't her school uniform.

I sucked some sauce off my thumb and said, "This pizza really sucks."

She laughed and dropped the crust that she'd been holding into the open pizza box. "So true. Why do we keep eating it?"

I lay back on Maggie's hood, stretching my arms up and placing my hands behind my head. Then I rolled to the side to face her and shrugged, a smirk on my lips. "Maybe you're doing it to impress me. But I have to tell ya, I'm only interested in friendship."

"Oh really? Just friendship, eh?" She looked at me with a disbelieving smile.

I nodded for emphasis, teasing her a little. "Really. Friendship and bad pizza."

"Well, my heart's really broken over that bit of news. You should have told me before I brought you out here to convince you I'm dating material." She laughed, nice and loud. It was the sweetest sound that I had ever heard.

"Too late now. Of course . . ." I reached out and pinched her jacket sleeve, giving it a gentle pull. "I might be able to be persuaded. It's been known to happen a time or two before."

"No. You seem pretty set in your ways to me." She tugged her sleeve from my hand and lay down beside me, looking up at the sky. She said, "The stars are pretty. See that constellation there? They call it the Northern Cross. It's supposed to be the image of a swan. Do you know much about Greek mythology?"

Sensing a make-out session wasn't on the agenda, I lay back and looked up. "Not as much as I should, I suppose."

"Well, the story about the Northern Cross tells of two close friends, Cygnus and Phaeton, who were constantly competing with each other. One day, they challenged each other to a race across the sky, around the sun, and back to Earth. But you know how competitive types can be." She paused, and for a moment, I wondered if she was referring to Grace and me. But then, it was always hard to figure out just what Caroline was talking about. "In order to gain the advantage, they both cut too close to the sun, and their chariots were burned up. They fell to Earth and were knocked unconscious. When Cygnus woke up, he looked for Phaeton, only to discover his friend's body trapped by the roots of a tree at the bottom of the Eridanus River. Cygnus repeatedly dove into the river, but couldn't reach his friend's body. While he sat grieving on the bank of the river, Cygnus begged for Zeus to help him. Zeus said that if he gave Cygnus the body of a swan, he would be able to dive deeply enough to retrieve Phaeton's body and give him a proper burial. The only catch was that if Cygnus did turn into a swan, he'd also have to give up his immortality and would only live as long as a swan would normally live. Cygnus agreed. And in honor of this great unselfish act, Zeus placed Cygnus's swan image into the night sky. Kind of a love story between the two of them, really."

I swallowed hard, now feeling like she could be talking about Grace or Josh. I wondered if she had any idea what had transpired between my best friend and me. Had someone seen? Were rumors spreading through the school that Josh and I had kissed? Absently, my fingers found my lips. What had it meant to him? What did it mean to me? And how would it affect our friendship? My voice caught in my throat for a moment. "That's so sad."

"No, it isn't. It's beautiful." She sighed, watching the night sky. "To think that someone could love someone else so much that they would give up everything for them."

"It must have been a hard choice to make."

"When it's love, I don't think the choice is all that hard at all. You just feel it. Even if it scares you. It's just there."

Suddenly, I realized that I didn't know what love was. Not the kind of love that Caroline was describing. Was that even real? Or just the stuff of fiction? Poets wrote about it. Singers sang about it. Hell, even scientists had theories about what was chemically happening in your brain. But did anyone really know what love was? Or was I the only one who had no real idea?

I stared up at the stars, fighting the bitter feeling in my chest from blooming any larger than it already had. I didn't know what love was. And not just romantic love, but the emotion itself. I'd moved from a family I couldn't recall to a foster home to a collection of people living under one roof. I thought I'd loved my parents, Viktor, and Julian. But what if I was wrong? How can you define a concept that's so ethereal, so untouchable?

What was I doing here? Not just with Caroline, but at Wills? I should have stayed in California. My being here certainly wasn't helping Viktor at all. And now things were complicated. With Josh. With Caroline. With Julian. With everyone. Maybe I should have stayed away. I lay there in silence for several minutes before speaking again. "So many of the stars are dead before we see them."

"There's a cheery thought."

"It's true. The light reaches Earth on a delay, and by the time it does, so many of the stars are already gone." I wondered how quickly all the light in my life would disappear. My parents, my friends, my dreams. My chest felt heavy. "Kinda makes you wonder why they bother shining at all."

We both grew quiet for a long time. Just as I was about to suggest that we head back to the dorms, she rolled on her side and looked at me. "You hate being here, don't you?"

"With you? Quite the opposite, actually." Of course I knew what she meant, but it wasn't like I wanted to talk about it, exactly.

But my brush-off wasn't enough to thwart her curiosity. "At Wills. You hate it here."

A sigh escaped my lungs and clouded the air around my face like a fog. "I do."

"Were you in such a funk at your school out in California?"

Lacing my fingers together, I laid my hands on my chest, feeling my lungs fill and deflate as I breathed. "No. But there were no reminders there of my past. I ran away from it all."

"Maybe facing it will be a good thing."

"You don't get it. I don't want to face anything. I can't get any of what I had back, and I don't even know if I'd want to."

"What bothers you more—that being here reminds you of your parents' deaths, or that your sister, Grace, is here antagonizing you still?"

When I spoke, it was through a clenched jaw. The evening had been ruined. What was supposed to be a night of light fun and hanging out had been tainted once again by Grace. "The two are intertwined."

"You think she had something to do with their deaths?" She paused, waiting for my reply, but I wouldn't respond. After a moment, she said, "Did you ever stop to consider that maybe your parents just had a terrible accident in the lab? It happens all the time."

"Not my parents. They were so careful." The heat of anger was making its way up my neck and cheeks. I wasn't angry with her, but at her insistence that we discuss my situation. It was nobody's business. Nobody's but mine.

"It's possible."

"No. It isn't." I sat up, more than ready to just call it a night. I didn't want to talk about my sister and what happened in that lab four years before. Right then, I just wanted to go to bed and forget about it for a while.

"Anything's possible." Her voice was so soft, but close. I closed my eyes, blocking out the stars, blocking out the pain, blocking out everything. Then I felt Caroline's lips against mine.

Her kiss was as gentle as her words, but like her words, there was something deeper behind it. I sucked her bottom lip gently and she pressed to me, slipping her tongue inside my mouth. Reaching up, I ran my hand over her hair, cupping the back of her head as we kissed. I imagined what it must have looked like from above us—two people, stretched out on the hood of an old car, linked in a way that I was certain I understood. It was all I wanted, that kiss. For the moment, it represented all that I had ever needed— acceptance, understanding, connection. When our lips parted, we looked at each other without speaking a word. Then she lay back down on the hood, and I joined her. We continued to gaze at the stars. After a long silence, during which I kept touching my lips with my fingertips in wonder, she spoke. Her tone was light, as if nothing intimate or surprising had just transpired between us. "You're a good kisser."

"Thanks."

"But don't get the wrong idea. I was just curious what it would be like."

I raised an eyebrow at her. "Kissing me?"

"Kissing. Period." Her words left me at a loss. What do you say to something like that? She looked up at the sky and sighed. "So many more are still alive, y'know."

"What are you talking about?" Being with Caroline was like hanging out with a living Rubik's Cube.

"The stars. You said that several are already dead by the time we see their light. But how many are still alive, still serving purpose, in comparison to those that no longer exist?" I wasn't sure if she was really asking, or if she was just being an optimist.

"Percentage-wise?" I cocked an eyebrow at her before looking back at the night sky. "Actually . . . over ninety-nine percent that we see are still functioning."

She turned her face toward me, her voice so low that I had to strain in order to hear what she was saying. "So why focus on less than one percent of what you see?"

She wasn't asking about the stars. She was asking about the cloud of pain and doubt that seemed to follow me no matter where I went. She was asking why I chose to see the glass half empty rather than half full. But it was more than that—to me, the glass wasn't just half empty. It was lying on the ground, broken into a hundred pieces, and would never be fixed again. Maybe it was a chemical imbalance in my brain. Maybe it was just my nature to be pessimistic and suspicious. I didn't have the answers, and there were too many questions. "I don't know. I guess it's easier for me."

"You look at all of those living, viable stars. But you refuse to see them. You choose not to. Just think about that." She sat up and hopped off of Maggie's hood. As she opened the passenger's side door, she said, "I'm tired. Take me home."

CHAPTER 13

PRESSURE:

A measure of how much push
something has exerted against it

The next morning, I took my time getting out of bed.

It wasn't like I hadn't kissed anyone before. And it wasn't like the kiss between Caroline and me had really meant anything, other than that we'd both been curious enough to experiment. But it felt weird seeing her the next day. Maybe it always felt weird seeing people the day after a kiss.

Of course, it felt weirder if you hadn't seen them for a couple of days after a kiss. Weirder still if they were your best friend. Y'know. Like Josh.

The first time I'd ever kissed anyone, they kissed me. It was my next-door neighbor, Kylie, when we were in the fourth grade. At the time, I thought it was pretty weird. I'd still thought it was weird two years later, when I kissed her older brother, Greg. Another boy named Greg kissed me at a sleepover that same year, which really made me question what it was about boys with that name. The next year, a girl named Sherry French kissed me after the seventh-grade winter dance. The irony of her last name and the fact that she'd put her tongue in my mouth didn't escape me. I could see the appeal of that kiss, despite the hygienic question of it all, and she was nice and everything. I guess I just never got bit by the dating bug enough to think that kissing was all that big of a deal. Boys, girls. It didn't seem like anything to go crazy over.

That is, if I'm being honest, until this weekend . . . when Josh had kissed me.

And really, kissing Caroline had been nice, too. Nice enough to warrant maybe kissing her again. If she was into that sort of thing. Maybe it would help me forget about how Josh's skin had felt against mine, or how I'd lain awake at night imagining what might have happened if I hadn't rushed out of the room the way that I did.

I should have stayed with him. And I was embarrassed that I hadn't. Maybe he was embarrassed, too. I didn't know. We hadn't spoken since.

I got another anonymous text message while I was

brushing my teeth, and it felt like a reminder that I wasn't supposed to be thinking about kissing at all. I was supposed to be thinking about what I'd found in Grace's lab.

I remembered how Julian had been on his phone when I'd gotten the texts on Saturday night. I couldn't let myself wonder if it had been Julian texting me this entire time, couldn't allow my imagination to slide down that rabbit hole. Julian had been a good friend and mentor to me, and a lot more than that to Viktor. The idea that he would somehow involve himself in some twisted game sickened me. And for what purpose? There was already a deep wedge between Grace and me. What purpose would it serve to add suspicion to the mix? What would Julian have to gain from such a thing? Nothing. At least . . . nothing that I was aware of.

After taking a colder-than-usual shower and dressing quickly, I made my way to the dining hall. Normally, I'd see Julian there getting a cup of coffee, but today he was conspicuously absent. Grace, however, was right on time and in her usual spot at the head table, surrounded by her friends and ignoring my existence. Seeing Carter, Taylor, and Ben with her sparked a feeling of dread, but mercifully, they seemed to be ignoring me, too. My stomach rumbled, but I was loath to eat anything heavy, so I finally settled on an apple and took a seat across from Quinn. He smiled as I sat. "You look like you hardly slept. Everything okay?"

"Yeah." I scanned the room again, but there was still no sign of Julian. "Yeah, I'm fine. Just a bit distracted today is all. Have you seen Julian around this morning?"

Quinn shrugged and pushed his glasses back up on his nose. "Not yet. But I heard a couple of the teachers are having some big meeting with the headmaster today. Several classes are going to be open study because of it. Why?"

"I just need to ask him something."

"Hey." Caroline walked by, as if nothing at all had happened last night.

All I could think to say was, "Hey."

Quinn watched her as she walked away. "She's . . . something."

I threw a surprised glance in his direction. "You like Caroline now?"

He shrugged, his cheeks blushing slightly. "Well, yeah. Kinda."

It was just a kiss, I told myself. It was likely nothing in the grand scheme of things. "You should ask her out."

Quinn looked quizzically at me. "I thought you two were seeing each other."

I blinked. What? Did everyone think that? Why? All we'd done was blow up a trash can and eat bad pizza. "No. We're just . . . friends."

"Give us a minute, would you, Quinn?" Josh seemed to

come out of nowhere. He sat on the edge of the table, dark rings under his eyes suggesting that he'd hardly slept. Every muscle in my body stiffened, then relaxed. It was just Josh. He was nothing to be afraid of.

Quinn raised his eyebrows at me but left without saying a word. After sucking in a deep breath, Josh said, "Look, Adrien. About Saturday . . ."

"What about it?" I forced myself to look him in the eye. How had I not noticed before what a beautiful shade of green his eyes were?

"I just want to apologize. I completely overstepped my bounds. I should have asked you." His voice sounded scratchy, like he'd been crying recently. A lot. I wondered if he'd also lain awake that night, thinking about me and what might have (would have) happened if I hadn't hurried out of the room. "I should have told you . . . about me."

I shrugged and smiled a small smile at him. "Well, you kinda did. In a really straightforward way."

His cheeks flushed, and he dropped his gaze to the table. He looked so full of shame, but didn't need to. "I mean . . . before."

Before. Before we'd kissed. Before his skin had touched my skin. Before our hearts had raced in sync with nothing but thin cotton between them. I swallowed, searching for the right words. Any words, really. "Well, I'd be lying if I said I saw it coming. I didn't. . . . I mean, I had no idea."

He locked eyes with me then, and a memory from kindergarten suddenly filled my thoughts. A pinprick on each of our fingertips. Pressing the blood together. Friends forever. No matter what. When he spoke again, it snapped me back out of the memory. "I'm so sorry. The last thing I want to do is wreck our friendship."

I shook my head. "Josh. Stop apologizing. It was . . . nice."

Now it was his turn to be surprised. His green eyes widened. In confusion, with a touch of hope. "Oh . . ."

"Yeah . . ." My cheeks felt warm. I didn't know exactly what I meant, except that I meant what I'd said. The fact was that the kiss had been nice. Nicer than kissing Caroline. Nicer than kissing anyone I'd ever kissed before. Hot nice. More-please nice. Don't-stop nice. When-can-we-do-that-again nice.

But I couldn't say those things aloud. Not yet, anyway. "I am still a little confused about why Grace was kissing you."

He sighed, the tension in his shoulders releasing some. "I took her to the booth for privacy. I wanted to tell her that I wasn't into girls. I thought that maybe knowing that would somehow make our breakup easier on her, y'know? But when I said it, she said she didn't believe me. Then she kissed me. It was . . . confusing."

A frown tugged at the corners of my mouth. "Grace never

was much good at taking no for an answer. You okay?"

He forced a smile. "As long as you're not mad at me, I'm fine."

"Why would I be mad?" I gave his shoulder a light slug. The corner of his mouth lifted in a smile. I couldn't help but think about how soft his lips had felt on mine.

Behind him, I spotted Julian and scrambled to my feet. "Oh shit. I've gotta go. Can we pick this up later?"

"Of course." He stopped me momentarily, putting his hand on my arm, keeping his voice low. His eyes seemed brighter than they ever had. "But Adrien . . . when you said it was nice . . . what did you mean, exactly?"

"I don't know. But . . . maybe we'll find that out together." Our smiles bloomed at the same time.

Julian had his arms full of books, and already he was walking in the direction of the exit. I called out to him, "Hey, Julian. Can I talk to you about something?"

He looked at me with the air of a very tired man, and he didn't stop walking. "Can it wait? I'm on my way to a meeting with—"

"No. It can't wait. It has to be now." It couldn't wait. I was done asking myself questions. I needed answers.

"Of course." He gestured to an empty classroom and we stepped inside. I closed the door behind us, and he set the stack of books he'd been holding on a desk before turning back to face me. "What's on your mind?"

So much. Too much. "How long have we known each other?"

He folded his arms in front of him and leaned against the desk, looking up slightly, like he was calculating in his head. "Oh, I'd say about thirteen years now. What's this about?"

"And in those thirteen years, I feel like we've gotten to know a lot about each other. I mean, you never talk much about your family or your past, but I always figured that was because you didn't get along with them or something. So we became your family. My parents, Grace, myself, Viktor. Am I wrong?"

"You couldn't be more right." Concern filled Julian's eyes, but it was very clear that he wasn't certain what he had to be concerned about. Not yet, anyway.

I took a step closer and glanced over my shoulder at the door to be sure that we were really alone. "I need to ask you a question, Julian, and I need for you to be completely honest with me."

He looked at the door, too, probably wondering who I thought might be lurking outside and why it troubled me so. "Always. You should know that by now. Now, what is it?"

"Do you trust Grace?" I was whispering now, but heatedly, the words burning my throat as I released them into the air. "Do you have any reason to suspect that she may have been involved in the lab accident that killed our parents? Truthfully now."

"Adrien." It wasn't a patronizing tone, but it was a parental one—one that made me question whether or not I had made up all of these possibilities in my anxious mind. He placed a gentle hand on my shoulder and leaned in close, his tone sincere. "Whatever it is that I may think or not think, all evidence points to the fact that what killed your parents was nothing more than an unfortunate accident. Bottles were mislabeled, and because of that, certain chemical compounds were misshelved. There is simply no evidence to support Grace's involvement. Now, perhaps even more important, what would drive you to think such things about your sister, and to ask me about what seems to be the day-dreaming of an overly anxious boy?"

"I've been receiving text messages from someone who seems to suspect Grace of wrongdoing." I took a deep breath, holding it in my lungs until my chest ached. When I spoke, it came out as a whisper . . . and a hope that I was wrong. "And I thought that someone might be you."

It pained me to see the hurt in his eyes. "Why would you think that?"

"Because when they texted me Saturday night, I saw you on your phone." Now that I was saying it out loud, accusing him right to his face, it sounded ridiculous. Julian was nothing if not loyal.

"It has to be a coincidence, Adrien. Nothing more." He furrowed his brow, shaking his head. When he spoke, he didn't sound angry, just troubled. Whether more for me or himself, I had no idea. "How could you think I would hide information from the police if I had it? I adored your parents, just as I adore you and your sister. If one of you did anything to harm them, I would report it to the authorities for your own good."

I pulled my phone from my pocket and typed in **Hello?**

Julian said, "What are you doing?"

"Texting whoever's been sending me these messages." I hit send and waited.

Julian withdrew his phone from his pocket and held it up for me to see. No text. Which meant that it hadn't been Julian who'd been texting me after all.

He met my eyes, his moistening out of concern. Maybe he thought I was going crazy. "I think that maybe you should talk to someone. Someone more qualified than me. A counselor, maybe. You've been different since your return to Wills. I think you might benefit from some professional help, Adrien."

I shook my head, but the argument that left my lips fell flat. "I'm not going to see a counselor."

"I'm just saying. All these years later, it seems like you haven't really taken time to mourn the deaths of your parents. Maybe it's time to face that, before it comes out in other ways."

"No offense, Julian. But I think this is a bit more than a communication teacher can handle."

Julian scoffed. "Maybe Mr. Wilson, the forensics teacher, would be better at answering your questions."

I snapped my fingers in revelation, and I turned to leave before he'd even finished speaking.

Julian's voice followed me out the door as I fled. "Where are you going? Adrien, I was joking!"

By the time I reached the forensics lab, I was out of breath. "Excuse me. Mr. Wilson?"

Mr. Wilson was a short, round fellow, with a pleasant face. He was wearing one of those tweed jackets with suede patches on the elbows, holding an open book in his hands titled *The Intricacies of the Human Brain*. When I whisked into his room, he looked up, snapping the book closed. "Yes?"

"My name is Adrien Dane. My parents were Allen and Claudia? They taught here a few years ago. Chemistry and botany."

"Dane . . . Dane." He looked up at the ceiling, as if the answers were written there. His eyes widened as his memory connected the dots. "Ahh, yes. Horrible fire. Lab accident, I believe."

"Yes." I swallowed hard, pushing the make-believe image of my mother's hand poking up from the ashes out of my mind. "I was wondering if you could answer a question about what was found at the scene of the accident."

"Well . . ." At first he hesitated, and I wondered if he thought it was a good idea to discuss such morbid details with the surviving child of two victims. Settling whatever he had to settle in his conscience, he said, "I'm not sure how much help I can be, but I'm willing to try."

"When I visited the house shortly after arriving, it looked like their lab had exploded and burned. Quickly, though. Because most of the house was untouched. Is there any way the explosion could have been caused by anything not chemical?"

"Well, there's always room for speculation. It sounds like an unusual scene, simply because of the amount of chemicals present. The fire could have started after the initial explosion, caused by an unfortunate combination of chemicals. I'm afraid it could easily have been a case of sloppy lab organization."

My jaw tightened and I shook my head. "My father was a brilliant chemist."

He leaned forward, locking eyes with me as his voice

lowered, as if his next words were for me and me alone. "Even geniuses make mistakes."

It couldn't be. It just . . . couldn't. When I spoke again, it was more to myself than to Mr. Wilson. "That doesn't make sense. My parents were meticulous about how they stored chemicals."

"Mislabeling happens all the time. Even in the most organized labs. I'm afraid the explosion was most likely simply an accident." He frowned and set his book on the counter. Before I walked back out the door, he said, "I'm sorry for your loss, and even more sorry that I can't put your mind at ease."

[CHAPTER 14]

ALLOTROPES:

*The different forms of an element that may
sometimes exist in the same state*

I found myself at the radio station, watching as Josh buzzed around the room doing DJ things. I merely sat on the couch, wringing my hands together, hanging my head. What was wrong with me? Was I right about Grace? Wrong? Was Julian correct and all these things were unfortunate coincidences? Was I losing my mind?

At one point, Josh pushed a button and removed his headphones before joining me on the couch. We sat like that through two songs—him sipping his weird mint tea with whipped cream, me just sitting and fretting in silence. Finally, he said, "Come on, man. What's wrong?"

When I spoke, my voice cracked. I felt like I was coming apart. "It's just . . . I thought I had the answers to a pretty important question. But I think I might be wrong. I think maybe it's all been in my head and I'm looking for answers where there aren't any."

Josh remained calm. He took another sip of tea and then set the mug on the coffee table. A hint of worry crossed his eyes. I was betting he thought I was regretting all the things I'd said to him regarding our kiss. "Can I know what the question is?"

There was a distinct division inside of me. On the one hand, I wanted to tell him everything. On the other hand, I didn't know who I could trust, or if I could trust anyone. Even myself.

But that was exactly why I had to say something to someone—and I could think of no one better than Josh.

"It's not about you and me, if that's what you're thinking. I just . . . It sounds crazy, but these past few days, being back here, I started to think maybe someone was directly responsible for my parents' deaths, like maybe they caused it on purpose. Y'know?" I swallowed the lump in my throat and added, "I thought maybe *Grace* had something to do with it."

"Grace? Come on, man. Your sister may be a lot of things, but a murderer?"

He met my eyes and nodded when he saw the seriousness in my expression. He gave my shoulder a squeeze. "Listen. If you really believed that, you wouldn't have waited four years to say anything to anyone about your suspicions."

"I guess." Shaking my head, I said, "That was before I was sure she was trying to pick up my parents' research herself. Plus, it was easier to not think about it all out west. Here, every day involves Grace in some way. Here, I can't seem to let it go, and the suspicious questions are just getting worse. What happened to that girl, Marissa, after she pissed Grace off? She had to go to the hospital from a *lab accident*. Then there's this secret work Grace is doing to continue our dad's research. And her attitude about my returning to Wills, pitting everyone against me? You might not have put those guys up to beating the crap out of me, but *someone* did. The evidence is all just supporting the same hypothesis."

"Look. Maybe those things *were* all accidents, or those assholes were just assholes. And maybe she really *is* continuing your father's work to honor his memory. Have you thought about that? Whatever you think about your sister, she's actually pretty brilliant. If she can do the stuff your dad was doing, why shouldn't she? Maybe all the nefarious stuff is in your head."

"Maybe." It was so difficult to believe. Things happened for a reason. Didn't they?

He sighed as he stood up. "Look, I need to get back to the job. Maybe we could hang out later or something?"

I nodded. Talking to Josh had always made me feel at least a little better. I was relieved to know that hadn't changed since we'd kissed. "Sure. Let's get off campus tomorrow after my chemistry test, head into town and find something to do. I could use a break from this place."

"Sounds good. Is this the tub explosion you've been going on about?"

"Yeah. It's gonna kick ass." The corner of my mouth lifted in a smile. Goddamn, I loved chemistry.

"See you tomorrow, man." Josh slipped his headphones back on and pressed a button on the board. "You're listening to Josh here at WILS. This next number by the Plain White T's goes out to Karen from Tre, who's really, *really* sorry about the other night."

The day had finally arrived. Mr. Meadows had gotten special clearance from the headmaster, the dean, and Coach Taryn. At no other school would "blowing shit up" qualify as a graded science project for a class. But then again, *Myth-Busters* made a lot of money blowing shit up in the name of science, so I guessed this was real-world training. And to be fair, we weren't really doing this experiment in class. We were doing it on the soccer field. Hence why we had to bring Coach Taryn on board.

The entire chemistry class, along with a few staff members, a representative from the school paper, and even Josh, who had managed to convince the radio station manager to let him do a live remote from the scene, lined the edges of the field. We were joined by members of the local fire department and EMTs, just in case. All were gathered to see the most amazing science experiment to hit the Wills Institute in many years—probably since my father had been a student. Either that or they were hoping someone would fail miserably, and they would be able to say that they had witnessed it firsthand. Naturally, Caroline and I were up first.

Our cast iron bathtub sat in the center of the field. Caroline was taking measurements to make sure that everyone would be standing far enough away so that they wouldn't be hit by any shrapnel. I sat on the side of the field going over the calculations for the experiment one last time. Too little potassium and we'd just get a fizzle, not an explosion—or a weak explosion like we'd gotten with the trash can. Too much, and someone could get hurt.

Caroline came up to me from behind, and her voice startled me out of counting when she spoke. "It looks like as long as no one passes the goal lines, they should be fine."

"Damn it." I started erasing the equation I'd been writing down. "Now I have to start all over."

Caroline grinned sheepishly. "Sorry."

"It's okay." I knew I was a little bit on edge. It wasn't her fault. "You just surprised me, that's all."

She put a hand on my shoulder. "Hey, you've done those calculations a zillion times. We're good. Don't worry."

I dropped my pencil onto the notebook. "Yeah, I guess you're right."

Caroline smiled down at me. "So, let's go blow up a bathtub, shall we?"

I stood up, and we both headed to the back of the truck that Mr. Meadows had used to transport all of the supplies to the field. "I'll grab the water buckets; you can get the potassium, okay?"

"Sounds like a plan." She picked up the jar filled with mineral oil and what looked like a silver stick of butter. I reached for two five-gallon buckets of water. "Besides, the potassium's lighter."

I shook my head and chuckled. "Shut up."

We reached the center of the field and I started to pour the water into the tub. Caroline set about placing the potassium into the triggering mechanism that she had designed. We had to make sure that the chemical wouldn't be exposed to the air or the water until everyone was at a safe distance, as potassium reacts with both. And while my father had taught me about chemistry, Caroline was the engineering mind on our team.

With everything in place, we were ready to go. I gave a brief presentation to the crowd about what they could expect to see and what exactly would be happening during the reaction, then I turned to my partner and asked her to do the honors.

Caroline reached for the remote that controlled the triggering mechanism, and that's when I saw it.

Caroline began to count backward. "Three."

The label on the potassium jar wasn't all the way centered. It looked like it had been removed and put back on—like there was another label underneath it.

The crowd counted with her.

"Two."

"One."

I dove at Caroline as her finger squeezed the trigger. The metal dropped into the tub.

I yelled, "Everybody get down!"

Time slowed as the mystery chemical was released from the clamps holding it in place. The silvery stick dropped into the pool of water with a splash. But before the droplets had time to settle back into the tub, an orange ball of flame began to grow from within the ripples.

The reaction was far more violent than what we had planned, which wasn't surprising, considering that all of our calculations were based on a different element. The bathtub was destroyed, just like Caroline and I had wanted. But the damage was far worse than we could have ever imagined.

Shards of hot metal and sparks flew through the air, hurtling toward the crowd of people. Screams were drowned out by the explosion. My body struck Caroline's and we tumbled to the ground. We landed with a thud, knocking the wind from my lungs. It felt like several minutes before I was able to breathe again, but in reality it was probably less than a second. The sudden intake of air into my lungs brought time back to its normal speed. Droplets of water and mud mixed with shards of broken and melted iron rained down from the sky. The air burned as I heaved in and out. I saw faces streaked with blood where students had been cut by shrapnel. Josh was pressing his right hand to a large gash on his forehead. I looked around from on top of Caroline at the crowd of people. At least I had managed to get her out of the way.

I could see the firefighters spring into action. Chemical extinguishers were already being sprayed onto the soccer field. The EMTs were treating people for their injuries. I looked down and asked Caroline if she was okay. That's when I saw the blood.

She moaned loudly as I rolled her over. A large chunk of metal was sticking out of her shoulder. I'd pushed her right toward the explosion when I'd tackled her. "What the hell?"

Her words were forced and, from the look on her face when she spoke, painful.

"Don't talk." I brushed a bloody lock of hair from her face. "Someone switched the labels. I don't know who or why, but I'm going to find out. You just lie here and I'll get help."

I screamed for the paramedics to come help, and I watched as they loaded her into the ambulance. I didn't even notice the cut on my cheek until one of them started working on me.

My head was in a fog. All I could think of was getting to that bottle. Someone had switched the labels, and I had a pretty good idea of who it was.

After returning from the hospital later that evening, I knocked hard on Grace's door. Fury and vengeance and all sorts of dark things were boiling up from within me and I planned to unleash them on my adoptive sister without regret.

There was no answer, so I tried the knob. To my surprise, the door swung open with ease. Lying on the floor was

Grace, her eyes closed. My heart raced to see her. "Grace? Are you okay?"

I hurried to her side and knelt down, pressing my fingers to her jugular. Her pulse was steady. What had happened? Had she passed out? She couldn't have been there long, or else surely her roommate or somebody would have found her.

I tried to scoop her into my arms, but the next thing I knew, a rag was pressed against my nose and mouth. A hand pressed it to me and in my shock, I inhaled the sickeningly sweet stench deeply. My head swam as nausea overtook me. Then my extremities began to go numb. Soon after, my vision and hearing failed as I fell into forced unconsciousness. My final thought before falling into that nowhere space was, *Chloroform. Someone used chloroform on me.*

[CHAPTER 15]

BINDING ENERGY:

*The amount of energy that holds
the protons and neutrons in the
nucleus of an atom together*

I don't know how long I was out, but when I came to, I was
sitting up, my head leaning back against a familiar surface,
my hands still numb, but behind my back. I pulled, but my
wrists seemed to be bound with something. Rolling my head
to the left, I realized that I was sitting in the driver's seat
of Maggie. The windows were foggy and it was dark outside.
To my right sat Grace. She was unconscious, but starting to
come to. I'd just opened my mouth to speak to her when I felt
something cold and sharp against my neck. A voice, familiar, but still too far away in my mind's fog to fully recognize,
growled into my ear. "Sit forward. And don't try anything."

I didn't know what other weapons he might have, whether he had accomplices or not, even what exactly was going on. So I sat forward and focused on my breathing, trying to get enough oxygen in my bloodstream to counteract the effects of the chloroform. At my wrists, I felt a small pull, heard a click, and realized that whatever had been tying my hands together—zip strips, I was betting—had been cut. My hands were still numb. Maybe from the chloroform. Maybe from sitting back against them for a time. All I knew was that I desperately wanted to shake them and get the blood moving again. But I didn't dare. Whoever had me—had us—meant business. I remained with my forehead on the steering wheel, my head turned toward my sister, asking too many questions to myself that I didn't have answers to. Who was this guy? What did he want? How on earth were we going to get free?

Grace's eyelids fluttered open and she blinked in my general direction. I couldn't be certain that she could make me out through the chemical fog, but I hoped so. I wanted to tell her to hold still, to breathe calmly and deeply, that everything would be okay. She would've called me out on that last one. I had no evidence that anything was going to be okay. I just didn't want her to be as scared as I was.

The shape in the backseat slid behind Grace and pushed her forward. In that same gruff voice, he said, "Stay sitting forward. Don't try anything. I have a knife, and I will slit your throat."

As my eyes adjusted to the darkness, I recognized the face of the man who was snipping the zip strips that held Grace's wrists. For a moment, shock filled me. Even if I'd known what to say, I couldn't form words.

All this time, I thought the person texting me had been Julian, knowing that he was as capable as anyone of tormenting me. For a moment, before I saw the man's face, I'd thought maybe Julian had figured out a way to get his hands on my parents' estate. Viktor's money might be going to Wills, but with Grace and me out of the way, our parents' money could end up going to him.

Only . . . it wasn't Julian sitting in Maggie's backseat.

It was Quinn.

As Grace's mind cleared, she looked at me, confused and frightened. I shook my head, but just barely, enough to tell her not to move, to do as he said until we figured out exactly what he wanted and how to get out of this situation without either of us getting hurt. Quinn gripped my hair and pulled me back until I was sitting upright in the seat. I winced but made no sound. The blade was at my throat again, Quinn's voice in my ear. "Oh, how I have waited for this moment, Adrien. It wasn't easy, you know. Living with you for days—*sleeping* in the same room. Apparently there was just nothing that would prove enough to make you kill Grace. I thought I had you pegged. But you proved to be a challenge."

He pressed the blade into my skin, and I felt my blood seep down my neck. It wasn't a deep cut, but it was enough to show me he meant business. "The thing about killing siblings is that if they die separately, it looks suspicious. Don't you think? So I started thinking about a way to do you both in together. A suicide pact would never be believed. You despise each other. A pact like that only works if both parties agree to it."

He was crazy. He had to be. None of this made any sense.

"Murder-suicide might have worked, but you just wouldn't cooperate." It sounded ridiculous. Like he thought he had perfectly logical reasoning and we were the ones being the problem. "Since you do all that you can to stay apart, I had to come up with something else. Something people would believe. A reason for you to be together. Same place. Same time. An accident."

He sounded so pleased with himself. "I'll tell the authorities that you blamed Grace for the accident at the soccer field. *I came along to try to stop him from doing anything stupid, officers, but he wouldn't listen to reason. Adrien dragged Grace into his car. They argued. It got heated. Adrien lost control of the car. I jumped out just before it went over the drop-off.*"

"What if we survive?" As I spoke, he pressed the knife in

deeper. Pain lit up the side of my face, my shoulder, my neck.

"You won't. Not according to physics. Neither of you will be wearing restraints. I've melted the locking mechanisms on the front doors. It's over seven hundred and fifty feet from the cliff to the bottom. I estimate a ninety-nine point seven percent chance of death."

"But . . . why? It makes no sense. Why kill us?" As I spoke, clarity returned at last to Grace's features. She looked scared. So was I. At last, we had something in common.

"I'd say money, but that would only partly be true. Let's just say it's complicated. Family matters usually are." He spoke the last words hotly into my ear.

"Family? What are you talking about?"

"Congratulations, children. It's a boy!" He cackled wildly, and as he did, he pressed the blade hard to my throat. As far as I could tell, the skin didn't split, but the pressure hurt. "It seems your father and my mother had quite the torrid affair several years ago. But when she told him the news of her pregnancy, he broke off all contact. My mother was threatened that if she ever told anyone who my father was, she'd regret it. Well, she did regret it, even with her sealed lips. You grew up with a trust fund. I grew up on a steady diet of ramen noodles and government cheese. It was bad enough knowing that I had a half sister out there, but learning that your father had adopted you, Adrien, when he didn't want anything to do with me . . . that really drove things home.

"My mother was a very fragile woman. *Was*. That's the operative word here." He grew quiet for a moment, and when he spoke again, it was from some far-off space, where only unstable psychotics ever visited. "We used to drive by your house. Sometimes she'd park the car and we'd sit outside, watching the lights inside turn off and on. She'd tell me stories about my father, and about the things she'd seen him do for my brother and sister. Birthday parties, trips to the zoo. It was her idea to get revenge. We deserved a little peace, a little happiness. So she taught me how to pick locks, and one day, she rang the doorbell. Your mother answered. Your father wasn't far behind. But the argument that ensued was just a distraction. I met my mom back at the car, after switching the labels in their lab."

My heart raced. "You son of a—"

Quinn pressed the knife in again, cutting off my words. "I thought revenge would be enough to bring her back to me, but it wasn't. She took her life three years ago. And that's when I began planning again. It worked out beautifully, volunteering at the hospital, and overhearing Viktor say that he was working to bring you home, Adrien. I was all too happy to help out with a few text messages, but that was even before I started following Grace. Oh, how the pieces came together." Quinn chuckled softly. "I wanted to see you feel the pain of losing your parents, Adrien. To suffer like I did. Before I took your lives."

He reached over and tugged Grace's hair hard. "In many ways, you and I are the closest relatives left in our happy little family, sis. And now, someone has to pay. I lost my mother because of our father's cruel, heartless actions. Now you'll both die."

Grace spoke up, her voice quivering some. "The autopsy. They'll detect the chloroform. You won't get away with it."

Quinn clicked his tongue. "You should have taken the forensics class. We learned that chloroform leaves the system relatively quickly after the person inhales oxygen for a while. There won't be a trace of it left by the time you go over the cliff."

I set my jaw. My shoulder was killing me. "And what makes you think I'll drive?"

"Because if you don't do exactly as I say, she'll drown in her own blood." Reaching around the seat, Quinn stabbed Grace in the lung and twisted the blade. Grace coughed up blood and immediately started to gasp for air.

Quinn looked at me then, his features sharp in the light from Maggie's dashboard. "She can die quick or she can suffer. It's up to you, brother."

My heart beat twice while I made up my mind.

"A quick death it is." I slammed on the gas, whipping

Maggie's steering wheel sharply to the right. Her front end was pointed straight at the cliff. I hit the gas hard again, all the way to the floor this time. The edge of the cliff was getting closer and closer. Maggie growled, ready for anything. Do or die. Together forever, baby.

Quinn took the blade from Grace's side and opened the back door. As he did, I whipped the wheel sharply to the left and slammed on the brakes. Grace's body lurched forward, smashing into the windshield. She bounced back into her seat, unconscious. My head felt wet and a bit like it was on fire. The steering wheel was covered in blood. I must have hit my head.

Maggie's back passenger's side door was open, and Quinn was nowhere to be found. My hands trembled as I opened the door and staggered out of the driver's side door. Skid marks in the grass led over the edge of the cliff. I approached carefully, trying to maintain my balance. My vision kept going in and out. Darkness, then stabilizing.

Clinging to a large rock just over the edge of the cliff was Quinn. As far as I could see, he was covered in blood. And laughing.

"What are you gonna do, Adrien? Kill me?"

I crouched down and stretched my hand out to grab him. "No. I'm going to save your ass and make sure you spend the rest of your life in prison."

Quinn grinned, his teeth rimmed in dark blood. "See you in hell, brother of mine."

Faster than I could take in a single breath, Quinn released his grip on the rock. All I could do was stare as he fell. I couldn't be certain, but it looked like he smiled the whole way down. Until he couldn't smile anymore.

CHAPTER 16

END POINT:

*A known pH point of an acid and base
interaction as shown by a chemical
indicator change in color*

The scar on my cheek had healed, but a fresh wound now occupied my entire being. Viktor's body, dressed in one of his favorite suits, was laying in a black coffin lined with purple satin at the front of the room. He had died peacefully in his sleep three nights before, five months after Quinn. After all my plans to return to San Diego, I'd remained at Wills. Even though it was just Grace and me now. And Julian, of course.

To my left sat Josh, dressed in a suit that made his eyes shine. He was quiet, but just having him there made me feel supported. Every once in a while, we'd exchange glances that told me that he was there for me when I needed him. And I did. More than he might ever know.

Caroline was sitting to the other side of Josh. Her wound from the explosion had healed long ago, and we'd spent more than a few nights sitting quietly on Maggie's hood, eating terrible pizza and watching the stars. She never made me talk about anything I didn't want to talk about . . . which is what good friends did, I supposed.

Several people had stood and said wonderful things about my godfather, but I found that words were lost to me. How can something as strong and profound as love be summed up in a mere few words? So I sat in the front row, watching as relatives, friends, neighbors, and colleagues approached the casket in a neat line to say their final good-byes.

I vowed at that moment that I never would.

I would mourn him, yes. I would miss him and think of him often. But I would never say good-bye to Viktor. Just as I had never said good-bye to my parents.

Julian had been busying himself playing host, making certain every guest had a drink or a napkin or whatever else they needed to keep his tears at bay. But his eyes were red. His cheeks were wet. There was no denying the agony that he had suffered from losing his best friend and husband.

I wondered if I would ever understand that pain. Maybe. Someday.

I reached up and straightened my tie, tightening the knot, the way that Viktor would have wanted me to. As I stared down at my freshly polished oxfords, I saw a pair of heels step up next to me. The wearer took her seat, and when I looked at her, there were no words.

Stretching my hand out, I cupped her hand in mine and gave it a comforting squeeze. The past, after all, was the past.

Grace laid her head on my shoulder and cried.

I brushed her hair from her brow and placed a gentle kiss there—the kind I'd always hoped our mother would give me in a moment when I'd needed comforting.

Grace said, "I'm sorry, Adrien. I'm so sorry. For everything. I was just so angry with you, so angry with Dad. That day we took the picture, I stole the pages from Dad's journal because I wanted to punish him. For playing favorites with you—for fighting with Mom. I don't know if he ever even noticed. I never got a chance to tell him I was wrong."

I put my arm around her and gave her a squeeze, whispering into her hair, "I'm sorry, too. But we're family. And we'll always have that."

As Julian stepped up to the podium, his eyes shimmering with sorrow, he unfolded the speech he'd carefully written the night before. He'd barely spoken Viktor's name when the dam inside of me broke and tears streamed down my cheeks.

The rest of the funeral was a blur.

ACKNOWLEDGMENTS

As people, we are constantly changing, growing, shaping into the best version of ourselves possible. Sometimes it feels like we are making these changes in a vacuum, all by our lonesome. But the truth is, we are surrounded by people who watch us change and grow and, if we're lucky, support us along the way. I'm very blessed to be surrounded by people who have had my back in more ways than one. These people—not all of them blood relatives, not all of them even human—are my family, in so many ways, and I owe them an enormous amount of gratitude.

Many thanks to the best damn editor in the universe, Andrew Harwell. If Hogwarts is indeed real, I know one day we'll find it together. You have no idea how much you have impacted my life and lifted me up. I'm so grateful for our friendship, and lucky to have you on my side.

My eternal gratitude to the most kick-ass agent in the literary world, Michael Bourret. MB, we've been together for over a decade, and every time I've stumbled or cried, you've picked me up and dried my tears. You are a true friend, a wonderful champion, and not allowed to stop being an agent ever.

So much love to my team at Harper. Rosemary, Kate, Olivia, all of you! Thank you so much for being so kind, so hardworking, so generous. My life would not be the same without you!

Huge hugs to my big sister, Dawn Vanniman, who has always been the voice of reason in my life. Dawn, when the world makes no sense at all, I can always count on you to raise an eyebrow with me. I love you.

Mad love to my Society Sisters and to every independent bookstore out there.

And of course, my deepest love, appreciation, and thanks go to the Brewer Clan. Paul, Jacob, and Alexandria— the three of you are home to me, no matter where any of us might be. You are my Elysia, my family, my friends, my saviors, and I would do anything for you. Just ask. I love you all more than anything in this world or the next (except for the kittehs . . . because kittehs . . .). Thank you for having my back, as always.

Last, but not least, thanks to my kittehs. Amenti Fang and Smudge—you've cuddled me when I needed cuddling, groomed me against my will, sat on my lap when I was trying to work, turned off my monitor when writing was frustrating me, and thrown up hair balls on my favorite rug. I can only assume that all of this means that you love me. I love you, too, my fuzzy lil masters.

And finally, a word of wisdom to my Minion Horde: Family is a word not reserved for those you are blood related to, but for those who fill your heart with joy. Thank you for being a part of my family.

TURN THE PAGE
for a sneak peek
at **ZAC BREWER**'s next book.

CHAPTER ONE

"It's a different color for you."

My mom was speaking with the same overly chipper tone she'd been using since she'd picked me up a few hours ago. She was trying to come off as supportive, but it was really ringing through my ears as fake. It was all fake. My new hair color, our casual conversation, the fact that I'd been released from Kingsdale Hospital with a "not crazy" stamp of approval. And I knew a thing or two about fake. I'd faked my way through six weeks of treatment with all the right words to all the right people. I'd convinced them all that I was in full-on recovery mode after what happened six weeks ago. But it was a lie. I was just trying to get out of that place, away from those white, sterile walls, even though I had no idea what it would be like once I did.

I only knew that I felt like a failure.

Staring out the window as Mom barreled down I-75 in the direction of our home, I thought about how, in a way, my life *had* ended that night in Black River. This—whatever this was—wasn't life. It was my afterlife.

"Yeah," I said. For seventeen years I'd had waves of strawberry-blond hair that hung to my waist. An hour ago, I'd had it dyed pink ombre. Part of me knew that I'd chosen that color to shove and poke at my mom's overly supportive act. She'd never let me dye my hair before. It had been an ongoing argument between us since I was thirteen. After four years of arguments, what had changed that suddenly made a surprise trip to the salon okay? Did she think that giving in to this one thing would somehow take back the guilt she might have over what happened? Ridiculous. So I'd chosen the most off-kilter color I could think of. I didn't even like pink. Or pastels.

Mom's phone buzzed as a text came through. To my annoyance, she picked it up with her right hand and continued steering with her left. I hated when she played with her phone while driving. It was so dangerous. People should never text and drive.

The irony that I was concerned about her endangering my life hit me hard, like a slap across the cheek. What did it matter, whether I'd drowned that night or smashed into a semitruck now because my mom refused to put her phone down while operating a vehicle? What made this so different from that?

Because, I told myself, *the river was my choice.* This was hers. And at least I wouldn't have taken anyone else down with me when I jumped into that water. It was just me. Just my ending. No one else's.

Mom said, "It's Ronald, wanting to know if you're up for seeing him this evening."

She and my dad were the only people on the planet who still called my best friend since kindergarten Ronald. Sure, it was his name. But ever since we watched that John Hughes movie *Pretty in Pink* together in sixth grade, he'd been Duckie to me. After a while he was Duckie to everyone. Just not my parents.

"I don't want to see anybody." I slid down in my seat a little. It was embarrassing. I was embarrassed. Not for having attempted to take my life. But for having failed. "I'm not ready."

She paused, biting her bottom lip, forcing down words that she clearly wanted to say. She started typing on her phone with her thumb before she even spoke again to me.

"Okay. I'll tell him." Her words were breathy and made me wonder what she was telling him exactly. My phone hadn't yet been returned to me, or I would have asked him. Of course, if I had my phone, Duckie would've just texted me directly.

She cleared her throat and said, "I think you should know, I've kept Ronald informed about your situation—"

Situation. Right. That's what it was. Just a situation. Nothing more.

"—so he's fully aware of your diagnosis and the treatment you're undergoing. I just . . . I just thought it might be good to have a friend involved."

Involved? Or an extra pair of eyes on me?

I'd thought about Duckie a lot since the doctors had given me a release date. I wondered what he thought about what I did, if he was mad at me for not telling him I wanted to die, why he hadn't come to see me on visitors' day. I was glad he hadn't come. I didn't want to have to smile at Duckie the way I smiled at my parents, the way I smiled at the doctors and nurses, the way I smiled all through the last few days of inpatient treatment. The truth was, I'd smiled my way out of the last six weeks at that damn hospital, but hadn't made any real progress. The truth was, I still wanted to die.

But I wasn't about to share that bit of information with anyone.

I'd learned early on during my stay in Kingsdale that their staff had pretty amazing bullshit detectors. If you tried to make light of things too soon, they only probed deeper, through the veil of your lies, to find the truth. I'd kept my mouth shut for the first week and observed. Then, slowly, I'd begun to act as if I were opening up, then growing hopeful, then regretful that I had thrown myself in the river. Eventually I convinced them that I was ready to face the world and wanted to change. I guess their bullshit detectors were off with me. I just wanted to be alone again so I could finish what I started. I just wanted to be free. Of the hospital. Of the pain. Of my life.

Dark stuff, maybe. But that didn't make it any less true.

My mom cleared her throat. It was as if she were attempting small talk with a stranger. Maybe she was. "Do you want anything from Starbucks?"

"Can we go home now, please?" I flicked the buckle on my backpack back and forth, not meeting her eyes.

She seemed relieved at my response. Maybe she wanted the tension in the car to evaporate and knew that going home would shorten our time alone together. Maybe I was way off base and she was glad I was engaging in conversation with her—brief as it was. I didn't feel compelled to ask, and I was tired of analyzing. I just wanted to get the initial steps of my return home over with already.

As we climbed a hill, I could make out Black River in the distance. I couldn't see the stone bridge, not from here, but it was there.

Instantly, I was transported back in time. I was seven years old. My dad was teaching me how to swim. As my head went under, I gulped in water, flailing my arms. I surfaced again, choking, and my dad pulled me out onto the deck of the pool. He looked so disappointed, so annoyed that I hadn't just swum. He said, "There's no reason to panic, Brooke. It's impossible to drown yourself."

But Dad had been wrong. With enough Tylenol PM, it was easy enough. In fact, if the old man who'd pulled me from the water hadn't seen me jump, I wouldn't be sitting in my mom's SUV now, still hurting with a pain that I couldn't explain or ease or wish away. I'd be gone. Somewhere better, maybe. Maybe nowhere at all. Just not here.

I reached inside my backpack and pulled out the prescription bottle with my name on it. The rattling of the pills inside briefly caught my mom's attention. She bit her bottom lip. I ignored her. The pills were white, with a black stripe and a green stripe wrapped around them. The doctors had called them antidepressants. They'd said that it might take several tries to find the right medication, the right dose. I was pretty sure they were full of shit. But I'd taken the pills at Kingsdale. Mostly because they watched me take them every day. I wondered if my parents would take over watching me from now on.

As I dropped the bottle back inside my bag, I looked at the three pink lines that marked my left arm. I hadn't been trying to reach my veins, to slash my wrists, to die in such a bloody way. It wasn't suicide then. Not yet. That was months before the night on the bridge. I'd just wanted to feel . . . something. Anything. Even if that thing was pain.

Of course, I was a total coward and couldn't get up the guts to just cut into my own flesh. So I'd downed some of Dad's scotch and tossed a couple of Mom's Vicodin down my throat and dulled the pain that I was longing to feel. Pretty stupid of me in hindsight. Made the whole thing pointless. Not that the experience had held much point anyway.

Word of advice: skin isn't easy to cut into. Not even with a brand-new box cutter. Not even when you apply a lot of pressure. I managed a few scratches at first. It stung, even through the dulling assistance of pills and booze. So I reached for one of my dad's chef's knives and resorted to sawing at my skin with its razor-sharp edge, pressing hard into my flesh until crimson bloomed. There wasn't a lot of blood, despite all my hard work and determination. And in the end I was left with three small scars on my arm—scars I explained away to anyone who asked as a clumsy accident tripping into tools in the garage. No one pushed the issue after I explained. Not even Duckie.

The cuts had healed relatively quickly, and had already begun to fade. But even if they faded entirely with time, they would always be there in my memory. Scars don't ever disappear—not really.

Mom turned the wheel, and we moved onto a familiar road. Two more turns and we were approaching our house. My stomach shrank painfully inside me. I had hoped never to see this place again. I had planned everything so well. I thought I had, anyway. But I hadn't planned on some nosy old man being out digging for night crawlers. I hadn't planned on a stranger intervening in the moment I'd been dreaming of, counting on for months.

We pulled into the driveway and "The Sound of Silence" by Disturbed came on over the radio. Mom killed the engine, cutting off the melancholy tune. For a moment, I didn't move, just sat there clutching the bottle of pills in my hand. I didn't feel sad or angry. I really didn't feel anything at all—apart from the determination to finish what I'd started at Black River. I was going to get it right the moment opportunity presented itself. And no one—not my parents, not Duckie, not some stupid old man—was going to stop me.

With a deep breath, I dropped the bottle inside my backpack and zipped it closed before I opened the car door. After I grabbed my suitcase from the backseat, I followed Mom up the front walk. The flowers out front had bloomed while I was in treatment. Shades of red, orange, and yellow greeted me as I made my way to the door with my backpack slung over my shoulder and suitcase in my hand. Their colors reminded me of flames.

Stepping inside the front door was like moving back in time. The floral paper covering the walls of the foyer seemed foreign to me, like something I'd once encountered in a dream. In fact, that's what the entire experience felt like: a bad dream.

I stared at the hands on the grandfather clock for a moment before moving deeper into the house. Time felt like it was dragging on, digging its claws in. My dad was sitting in his chair in the living room, reading the paper. When Mom spoke, her voice was more chipper than ever, bordering on shrill. "Look who's home, dear!"

Dad glanced up from his paper, but not at me. At the space between me and where Mom was standing. "Need help with your bags?"

He looked older, somehow, even though I'd just seen him two weeks before on visitors' day. The lines in his face seemed deeper. His posture slouched. I wondered if he was glad that I was home, but didn't dare ask. Shaking my head, I said, "No. I can manage."

With a crinkle of newsprint, Dad went back to reading

his paper without another word. I was more relieved than disappointed. Maybe this was his afterlife too. Just a blank haze of existence. Just an impending feeling of "get on with it already." Nothing more.

Mom shuffled her feet a little, wringing her hands as she stared at Dad. I didn't know what she'd expected him to do, greet me with hugs and smiles, balloons, and a Welcome Back banner? Frankly, I was glad I didn't have to face a conversation with him about what I'd done. I was far more comfortable with his silence than I was with Mom's false optimism. At least Dad was keeping it real. He was upset. And that was okay.

I carried my bags upstairs—each step seemed to make them just a bit heavier. When I reached the top, I looked down the hall to my bedroom door. The hall felt longer than I remembered, and as I moved toward my room, it felt like the distance lengthened with every step I took. The motion felt strange, wrong. Uneven, somehow, when matched with my presence.

I stretched out my hand and curled my fingers around the doorknob. Turning it slowly, I heard the click of the mechanism as it released. With a gentle push, my bedroom door swung open. My heart sank deep inside me, down to that dark place I'd called normal for so long.

The old man's words whispered through my mind—the

ones he'd spoken as he held me there on the riverbank after he'd pulled me from the frigid water, as the faint cry of approaching sirens grew. "You'll be okay, sweetheart. Everything's going to be just fine."

He was wrong. I wasn't okay then, and I still wasn't now. But I would be soon. Because, now more than ever, I was determined to die.

READ MORE
SINISTER PAGE-TURNERS FROM
ZAC BREWER

HARPER TEEN
An Imprint of HarperCollinsPublishers

www.epicreads.com

JOIN THE

Epic Reads
COMMUNITY